ANDREW JOHNSTON

BADGE OF EVIL

Complete and Unabridged

LINFORD
Leicester

First published in Great Britain in 2005 by
Robert Hale Limited
London

First Linford Edition
published 2006
by arrangement with
Robert Hale Limited
London

British Library CIP Data

Johnston, Andrew
    Badge of evil.—Large print ed.—
Linford western library
1. Western stories
2. Large type books
I. Title
823.9'2 [F]

ISBN 1–84617–321–3

Published by
F. A. Thorpe (Publishing)
Anstey, Leicestershire

Set by Words & Graphics Ltd.
Anstey, Leicestershire
Printed and bound in Great Britain by
T. J. International Ltd., Padstow, Cornwall

This book is printed on acid-free paper

BADGE OF EVIL

Lawyer Jack Langan left New York to travel out west to meet the father who had abandoned him. But he didn't expect to be offered the richest ranch in the territory — or imagine that he would be abducted. And he certainly could not have envisaged challenging the sheriff to a gunfight in front of an angry crowd of townspeople . . . For Langan to survive, he must discover his own courage and learn to understand the ways of the West.

1

'Franklin up ahead,' shouted the train driver as he watched the last piece of coal being thrown into the furnace. He pulled the cord above him and the shrill whistle also proclaimed the journey's end.

The Utah Northern Railway had recently been extended into Idaho Territory and still carried mainly freight that would be loaded into wagons and taken as far north as Montana. Only one passenger disembarked from that afternoon train. He laid his dirty brown canvas bag on the station platform and rubbed his hands into his face. Unshaven skin reminded him that he had spent a full two days travelling. His body, almost six and a half foot tall, had not been designed to fit into those cramped restricting seats and he felt sore and uncomfortable. As he placed both hands on his spine and arched himself backwards as far as his frame would permit in a satisfying and releasing stretch, he looked skywards. But his eyes were forced almost shut, for the glare of the summer sun of 1883 was fierce even this late in the day.

Through his squint he could see the sign indicating the Hotel Metropole on the other side of the broad dusty street. He instinctively reached for the letter folded up in his inside jacket pocket. He knew that this was the establishment to which he had been directed but still his legal training compelled him to check. When the crinkled note confirmed that he was looking at the right place, he grabbed the bag and strode out of the station. He wanted a wash, some food and a good stiff drink. He would not be perturbed if they were not secured in exactly that order.

The hotel clerk, a short bald-headed man in a flamboyant green-and-red waistcoat, looked up as he approached. He made a note of the fine grey suit, trilby hat and brown leather shoes. These proclaimed in a booming voice that his visitor was not from around these parts but he smiled when he saw that the man was carrying no sidearms.

'Hello there, stranger. What can I do for you, today?'

'Name's Langan, Jack Langan.'

The smile behind the counter widened.

'Yes sir, Mr Langan. Been expecting you. We have a room for you, finest in the hotel. Booked by Pat Langan. In fact his man, Edmund Clay, was in just yesterday to check that everything was in order. They sure seem keen to see you. You related to the other Mr Langan, or somethin'?'

Langan understood that in this small town where few strangers passed through curiosity would not be confined to a check-in desk. He decided he would provide some brief details in the hope that this might prevent further speculation or intrusive questioning.

'He's my father,' he noted sharply, as

a quizzical look spread over the other man's face

'Your father? Well, my goodness. I've known Pat Langan for as long as I can remember and he's never talked about having a son to me.'

'It's been quite a while since I talked about him. So I guess that's us about quits.'

Langan accepted the key that was being proffered and retrieved his bag. His expressionless face provided solid evidence that any request for further information would be regarded as unwelcome. The clerk understood.

'OK. None of my business, I guess. You are in room 16, Mr Langan. Anything else we can do for you? Pat insisted that we make sure you have everything you need. Anything you want, you just ask me. Name's Milo. Pat said to tell you it was all on his account.'

Langan had started to move away but this last statement caused him to stop. He spun around and with an unexpected venom hissed:

'I'll settle my own account when I leave, but you can send someone up with a bottle of whiskey and a glass.'

Finding the comfort of sleep had been difficult for Langan since his wife died from consumption ten years previously. He had lain drunk on the street that night and the demons born out of this guilt regularly haunted him. But for now he was anaesthetized by the heady concoction of alcohol, fatigue and stiffness. His feet hung over the end of the bed but this mattered little. He had barely awoken the following morning when he heard the sharp knock at his door and answered it, protecting his modesty only by a towel around his waist. In front of him stood a large black man, a few years younger than himself, with a shotgun cradled into his arms. The gun was broken and the barrel hung limp down his side but Langan still was left with a distinct sense of menace.

'Mr Langan's downstairs waiting for

you. He don't like being kept waiting.'

'You Edmund?'

'That's right. But we can save the formal introductions for later 'cos as I say Mr Langan is waiting.'

'Well, he's kept me waiting for over thirty years and I'm afraid he's going to have to wait a little bit longer. I'll be down when I'm good and ready.'

Then the door was slammed with a resounding bang. Edmund jumped back and snapped the gun shut but when he realized the futility of continuing to point it at a closed heavy door, he sheepishly withdrew. He ambled slowly downstairs and crossed the lobby into a large parlour. At the far end, sitting at one of the many low tables was an old tired-looking man. His hat lay in front of him and he was casually rubbing the felt, deep in expectant thought. Edmund agonized over how he would tell his boss that he had failed to deliver the summons with which he had been entrusted just a few minutes earlier. His concern, though, was misplaced for no sooner had he started to relate his encounter, when out of the corner of his eye he saw the intended recipient approach. Pat Langan immediately stopped listening to his employee and stood up to thrust a handshake towards the tall, strangely dressed figure.

'Howdy son. It's been a long time. You were only fifteen when I saw you last but I still recognize you. Sure do. You've turned into a mighty fine man and a lawyer as well. I'm proud of you, son. Glad you could make it all this way. Pull up a seat, son, beside me and I'll get Edmund to fetch us some coffee.'

Langan looked at the old man, stooped now with age but still greater in height than most. He had a shock of white hair brushed backwards over his head. Langan's eyes were drawn to the broad gun belt slung around his waist and the two holstered pistols with mother of pearl handles protruding backwards like angel's wings.

Tentatively he placed his hand in the

outstretched palm.

'Don't you dare call me 'son', ever again,' he whispered. 'You surrendered the right to be my father when you walked out. Jack will do just fine.'

An uneasy silence hung in the air till Langan threw a surreptitious nod in the direction of Edmund to indicate that he could leave. As soon as he was gone, father and son sat down.

'OK. Jack,' the old man said. 'I appreciate that you are angry about what happened and I don't blame you. But I'm an old man now and the doc has told me that the ticker is getting pretty weak. There's not that much longer to go now. I want to square things up before I leave this world. I want to tell you why I never came back.'

'I don't need to know that. Not now. Not any more,' Jack growled. 'After you left Mom took over. She worked fourteen hours a day, cleaning houses for the rich people in the Upper East Side and then walking back to the

Bowery to make sure I had eaten each day. She continued working to put me through law school and I promised myself that I would repay her every last red cent. But, of course, I never got that chance. Poverty drove her to an early grave while you were out here.'

The mention of his first wife pulled a watery film over the old man's eyes. Jack could see that the old man was struggling to hold back a tear as he replied in softer tones.

'It wasn't like that, son. In the beginning I tried to send some money back each month to your mom. You never knew it but every now and again she would write me a little note telling me how you were doing. I heard all about you starting law school. Sure, that's how we tracked you down to send you the letter. I asked my attorney here in Franklin to find out where you were working. Henry tells me that you are a partner now in that fancy law firm. I never really abandoned you, Jack. I thought about you most days, wondering how you were doing.'

'Why did you not come back and find out?'

'Well, life goes pretty quickly the older you get and time just started to run out. There was always something going on, building up the ranch, protecting the place during the Sheep-eater Wars. They brought the railway up here in seventy-nine and I sure as hell thought about it then. But by then things were starting to go wrong between Rebecca and me.'

'Rebecca?' the younger man repeated in a questioning tone.

'Yeah, my wife. In fact she was the real reason I never came back. She was working in the saloon and she was the prettiest young thing you ever did see. I fell head over heels in love with her and all the money that I had saved to take back to New York, I used to set up a home for her. That was Far Fields. It's one of the biggest cattle ranches in Idaho, now. Then we eventually got married after I learned that your mom had passed on.'

Langan looked disdainfully at his father who had no difficulty comprehending the meaning of the expression.

'I'm not a bad man. Believe me,' he pleaded. 'It became pretty hard back East in 1850, you know. We had had not too bad a time up till then. The Irish were recognized as good workers. Then every day a new shipload of immigrants would disembark, more Irish, Poles, Italians and Germans. Each one would sell their labour for five cents a day cheaper than the one before. I was fit and strong, just like you are now. And I wanted to work but even when I was lucky enough to find a job, I couldn't make enough for the three of us to live. So your mom and I agreed that I would come out here to the frontier and drive the steers until I had saved money to make something good, to break free from having to queue up on the quayside every morning to beg for work.'

The ageing rancher ran his fingers

through his thick hair and then leaned forward towards his son to proclaim: 'I've only ever loved two women in my whole life, your mother and Rebecca. You know, Jack, that when love hits a man it's like bein' run down by a whole herd of steers. That's how it was the first time I saw Rebecca. I just couldn't go back East and leave her. I'm really sorry for what it did to you and your mom but there was nothing I could do. I didn't come out here looking for another woman. It just happened. Life would have been much easier if I had just wanted to bed some cheap bar-room singer but I really did love her. And there has never been anyone else since.'

Jack was smiling a discreet smile at his father's persistence not to be seen as some ageing Lothario when Edmund reappeared with the coffee. The cups were being set out as Jack asked:

'Your new wife, Rebecca. Am I going to meet her?'

The sound of Edmund dropping the

coffee-pot on to the table caused father and son to recoil in their chairs and then jump up but still the warm brown liquid splattered over both of them. They were wiping it off with their hands as Edmund apologized profusely.

'That's OK. Don't worry about it. It was only an accident. Why don't you go and get us a few towels,' asserted his boss.

As Edmond negotiated his large frame through the intricate maze of low tables, the two men sat down again.

'Guess Edmund just came in at the wrong time and was spooked by that question,' Pat explained. 'As I said we had a kind of rough patch and I threw her out. Built her a brand new house though at the far end of the ranch. That shows you how much I loved her. She lives there with her maid, Maria. There has always been young bucks sniffing about. Couldn't blame them, she was so darn pretty but she didn't need to encourage them. I guess I put up with it because I was so much in love with her.'

'You said 'was',' interjected Jack.

'That's right. A man can only put up with so much before he snaps. I just couldn't stand the idea that she was seeing someone behind my back.'

'So you going to get a divorce?'

'You are a lawyer. You will understand this. I've no grounds to divorce her. I have plenty of suspicion about her infidelity but no proof and she realizes that I am not a well man so she is intent on sitting things out, knowing that she will inherit the whole of Far Fields pretty soon. At least that's what she thinks but I ain't about to let her put one over me like that.'

Edmund returned with two large white cotton towels but caught just enough of the conversation to understand that he should merely deposit them on the table and tactfully withdraw. He saw, however, a face flushed with embarrassment when Jack responded:

'I'm sorry, I didn't mean to pry. It's no business of mine.'

'Ah, but it is, Jack,' corrected the old man. 'You're my only kin now as far as I'm concerned. And at the end of the day, blood is thicker than water. That's the main reason I sent you that letter asking you to come out here.'

The puzzled look requested elaboration and his father acceded. 'I want to change my last will and testament to ensure that you get everything, save for a few hundred dollars to make sure Edmund is all right. That means I want to leave Far Fields to you. How would you feel about giving up pencil-pushing and becoming a rancher? I mean a seriously rich rancher.'

2

Sheriff Billy Bob Hickey and his three deputies, Peter, John and Little Bob were all brothers or half-brothers and hence rejoiced under a common surname. Their shared ancestry was defined through their father who had held the position of sheriff prior to Billy Bob. Insult or injury to any one of them was collectively viewed as an attack not just on the authority of the law but also as an offence against the family. So when Mitchell, the miner, swung his long-handled spade at Peter and knocked him clean to the ground, they all understood that retribution would be required and that it was Billy Bob's responsibility to give clear direction as to how it should be executed.

The four of them had ridden up to the mine-workings that morning because they knew of Mitchell's reputation as a man who could handle himself. He had frequently been involved in scrapes in town and more often than not he would have been the instigator. But until this point it had always been with other miners and Billy Bob was content to let them settle it themselves as long as it didn't interfere with the business of the God-fearing townsfolk. In fact their fights often provided interesting entertainment. But last night had been different. Mitchell, when refused more drink, had head-butted Jess Patton, owner of the Silver Dollar saloon and to the sound of a resounding crack broke his nose. Then, somewhere between the bar and the boardwalk, he remembered that he had walked into town that day and the prospect of a six-mile walk back to camp in the dark, and in his state of inebriation, did not appeal. So when he saw the saddled horse tethered up outside the saloon it provided the obvious solution.

Horse-stealing was a most heinous offence in the sheriff's eyes and he had determined very quickly that Mitchell would have to be brought in to face justice. Keeping the rule of law was not just a case of retribution; it was also a case of making examples of miscreants so that others would think twice before they embarked upon similar actions.

When they reached the miners' camp they saw the missing mount tied up outside one of the tents, still with its saddle on its back. Billy Bob spat on to the ground the remnants of the strands of tobacco that he had been chewing for most of his journey up there before calling out Mitchell's name. After a few minutes a bleary-eyed, hung-over half-dressed figure emerged. A group of miners formed a little audience around the anticipated theatre.

'Mitchell,' cried the sheriff from the saddle of his horse, 'you know that you are going to have to come back into town with us, don't you. I don't want any trouble, so just you behave now. You hear me, boy?'

The miner stood in silence and Peter dismounted with a set of iron shackles. He was bending down to put on the ankle-chains when Mitchell shouted out.

'Hell, Sheriff, that ain't necessary. I know I've done wrong and I'm coming back.'

Peter momentarily stopped and waited for guidance.

'I'll tell you what's necessary and what's not. The leg-irons are going on,' provided the sheriff.

He had just resumed the shackling when Peter saw Mitchell grab the spade and swing it through the air. The force of the blow to the side of his face threw him through the air and as he landed he cowered in anticipation of another strike. Mitchell was standing above him with the spade raised when the noise of three pistols being cocked caught his attention. He quickly assessed the odds and knew that the Hickey boys would have absolutely no compunction about shooting him down like a dog as long as he continued to pose a threat to one of their number. He threw the spade to the ground and raised his arms in a gesture of surrender. The lawmen dismounted and Little Bob finished the task of restraining the prisoner while the sheriff never let the aim of his pistol waver from the miner's head.

As soon as John had helped the groggy Peter to mount up, they set off with their prisoner staggering on foot, roped to the rear horse. The leg-shackles meant that Mitchell could proceed only by slow shuffles and as soon as they were out of sight of the miners' compound, the lawmen would take turns to tighten the rope and drag him along the ground. Then they would stop and pull him back to his feet for the process to be resumed over and over again. Only John showed little enthusiasm for this sport. After about an hour the party decided to stop for some victuals. Mitchell was grateful for the respite but was thrown unceremoniously against a tree a few feet away from where the fire was being made. When the law enforcement officers had finished eating, Billy Bob sidled up to the bruised and battered miscreant. He removed his pistol from its holster and gestured with short jerking motions but when they failed to transmit the intended message he emptied his mouth of his chewing tobacco.

'Stand up, boy,' he shouted. 'On your feet when I'm talking to you.'

Mitchell painfully pulled his body to a standing position and the sheriff spoke again. 'You hungry, Mitchell? You want some stew?'

'Sure do, Sheriff. That's mighty decent of you.'

'Oh, I forgot, it's old man Langan's meat. It's kind of tough so you would need a good set of teeth to chew it up proper like.'

'I got a good set. I'd be all right.'

'Show me, Mitchell. Show me and I'll work out whether they're sharp enough.'

Mitchell opened his mouth in a grotesque grin and Billy Bob's hand flew through the air until the butt of the pistol smashed into the prisoner's mouth. The taste of warm blood was intermingled with the grit of broken teeth.

'Nope, I doubt very much whether you could chew that chuck.'

The deputies were still laughing at this last remark when Mitchell was hit again on the shoulder with the handle of the gun. He closed his eyes in a painful grimace and when he opened them again, his vision focused on the three men walking towards him, each wielding a pickaxe handle. He lifted his manacled hands to protect himself but it was to no avail. Heavy, sickening, merciless blows rained down until he passed out. When he came to, he was being laid over the spare horse and bound hand to foot under its belly. His body ached all over and he could see the black-blue of bruising covering his arms without interruption. His mouth was full of blood, which he coughed out. He knew instinctively that this was not just blood from the broken teeth but also haemorrhaging from more visceral locations. It would continue to be propelled into his gullet and he had to stay awake to spit it out otherwise he would drown in that warm red liquid that was the very essence of his life. Amongst the raucous laughter he heard voices.

'Heh, look he's coming around again.'

'Yep, he's a strong one. You never know, he might just pull through.'

'Naw, he'll be dead, before tomorrow morning. Just look at the state of him.'

'Five dollars say he makes it.'

'No doctor till then?'

As the procession moved off, Mitchell heard Billy Bob's opinion on the wager.

'Dead or alive. It doesn't really make

that much difference. Horse stealing's bad enough, but for resisting arrest and then trying to escape custody, the county judge will want him strung up.'

3

Had the full quartet not gone to apprehend Mitchell, they would have made it their business to meet the train the previous day. They would then have seen the stranger who had arrived in their midst and duly discovered his identity. The sheriff liked to pride himself on the notion that he knew everything that was happening in his town but as they congregated at the jailhouse that morning they were totally unaware of the reunion that was about to take place.

Peter entered the small confining cell and pulled the rough horse-blanket away from the prisoner. He knelt down at the bench and after a few moments shouted out.

'He's still breathing alright. Told you he was strong. That's five dollars you owe me.' Little Bob cursed under his breath on the other side of the bars, but the sheriff cut across further discussion.

'Seems like living is more important to Mitchell than we thought. Wonder what's so good about his miserable existence. Better give him some help if he's so scared of dying. Bob, you run over the street and fetch Doc Morrison.'

Morrison came over just a few minutes after Little Bob returned. He was shown straight into the cell where he started his medical examination. He looked up.

'This is an abomination,' he barked. 'What in heaven's name happened to this man?'

'He tried to escape, Doc. Seemed to forget he was wearing leg-irons and went straight over some sort of cliff. Must have fallen a good twenty feet into an old quarry.'

Morrison shook his head with a look of resigned disbelief and disparagement. Silently he expressed disgust at the sheriff's notion of justice but was too frightened to give any vocal expression to that view. He understood that his ministrations would in all probability be in vain but when they were complete, the doctor packed his case and prepared to leave. Little Bob stood in the doorway letting his eyes follow the medic as he crossed the street. The lawman did not hear the curses that were coming from under Morrison's breath but his attention was seized when a cavalry officer stopped his horse directly in front of the jailhouse. He watched the stranger tie up his mount on the wooden rail that ran along the boardwalk.

Little Bob knew that a visit from the military was never good news. They always wanted to interfere on how the sheriff ran the town. He had heard the sheriff say over and over again that just because the politicians down in Boise were preparing a case to get Idaho admitted into the Union, it shouldn't mean that some little kid still wet behind the ears and straight out of West

Point could dictate to the sheriff what he should and should not do.

The blue-serge jacket and grey jodhpurs were covered in dust, betraying the fact that it had been some time since this soldier had left his base. The lieutenant wiped his forehead with a neckerchief and then almost instinctively started to polish the crossed-sabre badge on the hat that he was holding. As he rubbed the insignia he became aware that he was being observed.

'I'm Lieutenant Nichol,' he said, as he caught Little Bob's stare. 'I'm looking for Sheriff Hickey. Told I could find him here.'

Little Bob did not utter a sound but merely turned towards the sheriff and his brothers. They, in turn wanted to know what had captured Little Bob's attention so suddenly.

'What is it, Bob?' demanded the sheriff as he wrenched the door of the jailhouse from the bemused deputy's grasp. He also stopped as soon as he saw the blue uniform. Nichol repeated his introduction and Hickey beckoned him inside with the words:

'I'm Hickey. What can I do for you, Lieutenant?'

Nichol saluted perfunctorily and then unfolded a rolled-up parchment map before laying it out on the sheriff's desk.

'Need to brief you, Sheriff, on the movements of some wayward Shoshone Indians. We believe that five braves left their reservation about a month ago and are prowling about in this area. They were seen a few days ago by a fur-trader up around Blackies Canyon, here.' His index finger landed on the parchment.

'I've been sent from Fort Douglas to find out what's going on but the platoon's been unable to find any other trace of them so far.'

'Blackies Canyon is part of Far Fields, old man Langan's lands.'

'Has he been in recently reporting any stolen cattle?'

'No, nothing like that at all. But then Langan likes to see himself as a sort of independent man. I guess that even if he was aware of missing steers he'd try to track them down himself. You want me to ride on out there and have a word with him?'

'Be obliged if you would, Sheriff. Platoon is down at the big bend in the river. We are going to pitch some tents and take a couple of days' rest there. Horses and men are both plumb tuckered out. So you can catch us there.'

As Nichol started to refold the map, Little Bob asked the question. The same question that was meandering around the minds of the rest of them but without finding a path to their lips.

'These Indians, Lieutenant, they likely to be dangerous? They gonna be scalp-hunting?'

'Shouldn't think so. They are more likely to be hungry. But I doubt whether they would attack a white man unless they were really cornered. They understand now that they have to abide by the law.'

'Yeah,' agreed the sheriff. 'We sure as hell learned them that lesson at Bear River.'

Nichol pulled himself upright and his face started to turn puce with anger.

'Sheriff, Bear River was twenty years ago. The Shoshone nation has put it behind them. It was a dreadful mistake.'

'Mistake? It wasn't a mistake. It was us laying down the law to these varmints.'

'Those varmints as you call them,' snapped Nichol, 'were two hundred and fifty unarmed men, women and children that we massacred. We should be grateful that the Shoshone are noble enough to put that behind them and sign peace treaties.'

He confirmed the arrangements regarding Langan and marched out of the jailhouse, concealing his anger to the best of his ability.

4

Jack agreed that since no eastbound train was due in Franklin for the next few days he would spend some time on the ranch, irrespective of his decision on the offer with which his father had surprised him. They rose from their seats and Pat dispatched Edmund over to the livery stable to start getting the buggy ready. As they walked through the hotel, Jack Langan continued to protest that he would be completely unable to accept the bequest. But the older man dismissed all of these objections with a wave of his arms.

'Hell, Jack. I know that you were not looking for anything when you came out here. Henry Woods gave me a fair idea of what you are earning as a lawyer back East. I know that you are not short of a dollar. But I am talking about more money than you would earn in two lifetimes.'

Just before they went through the door and into the street, Pat added: 'And with the railway coming through you could sell Far Fields meat coast to coast. That's another reason I want to pass the ranch on to somebody like you. Somebody with a business brain. Somebody who will continue my work building the place up.'

They both failed to notice Milo looking up and opening the mental notebook that he always kept handy for information such as that.

As Edmund proceeded to the livery stable he passed the jailhouse and saw the four lawmen standing outside. The silver badges that they all wore on their chests were glinting in the sun. Edmund cast his eyes downward in the hope that that would make him inconspicuous. At first the brothers were focused on ensuring that Lieutenant Nichol was indeed leaving town but then Peter spotted Edmund.

'Billy Bob, there's Langan's man,' he

called out. 'Never knew that he was in town today.'

The sheriff removed a stick of tobacco from a pouch and with his knife cut off a small knob of the brown rod. He put it in his mouth and it started to soften when his saliva was mixed into it. They crossed the street and Billy Bob placed himself directly in Edmund's path. The others formed a small threatening circle behind him.

'Well, well, Edmund. You been sent to run errands or is old man Langan with you today?' mocked the sheriff.

Edmunds responded in what he hoped would be perceived as a tone of due deference but also emphasized his employer's title.

'Yes sir, sheriff. Mr Langan will be comin' down the street very shortly.'

'So what brings him into town?'

'That's Mr Langan's business, Sheriff. You would have to ask him yourself.'

'Don't give me your lip, boy. You are forgetting who you're speaking to. I got an important message for him from the military.'

'I ain't givin' you no lip, Sheriff. As I say, sir . . . '

But Edmund could say no more before the sheriff pushed him over the kneeling Peter. As Edmund's back thumped on to the wooden slats, his rifle fell beside him. He instinctively stretched out to grab it but heard the sheriff's cry tear through the air.

'Don't even you think about it boy.'

Edmund looked up, straight into the hollow metal tube that was the muzzle of the sheriff's pistol, but the shout from down the street caused them to postpone further discussion. Pat Langan had sprinted when he saw the lawmen crowd around his foreman and was out of breath when he reached the scene. He pulled a large draught of air into his lungs.

'Leave him alone, Hickey,' he wheezed. 'Let him up.'

'So, Langan, you come to protect your boy?'

'He's more of a man than either you or your simpleton in-breeds will ever be.'

Hickey turned to face this insult square on, his eyelids pulled tight not only by the strength of the light but also by the hatred that he harboured for the man now in front of him. Langan stopped talking. The sheriff's fingers twitched over the holsters of his pistols like two squirming spiders.

'You ain't not to have said that, Langan. You have gone and upset my deputies.'

Pat Langan brushed aside the tail of his coat to reveal his own brace of Colt .45s. He stood staring at the sheriff and Langan saw in the old man's eyes a steel that had been forged in the white-hot flames of determination and courage. He suddenly remembered that he had seen that look before. Almost two decades previously: the first gun-fight that he ever witnessed. It had been in the saloon, before Langan and Rebecca got married. She was still singing when one of the gamblers seated at a table in reach of the small dais that acted as a stage pulled her over to his seat and then forced her on to his knee. From the back of the room Langan marched across and asked him to leave her alone, but the gambler ignored the request and waved his hand peremptorily to dismiss the objector. As Langan pulled her away, he took the gambler's seat from under him with a sweep of his foot, crashing him to the floor. Everyone was laughing until the gambler got up and shouted out that he was going to kill Langan. The room went deadly still; Langan pushed Rebecca away and then turned around to face his adversary. He had already learned enough of the ways of the West to take threats like that seriously. That was the moment when Hickey had seen the same look that was in front of him just now.

The gambler had only started to level his pistol by the time that Langan had drawn, aimed and planted a bullet directly in the middle of his chest.

Twenty odd years, thought Hickey, must have taken his toll on the man's reflexes. But he knew that he would not be able to gauge with the same accuracy as Langan's shot, the rate of deterioration. A bead of sweat crept insidiously out onto his forehead.

'Don't be a fool, Langan. You are too old to pick up gunfights any more. Your eyes have gone. Your hands are shaking.' The sheriff smirked and concluded: 'And even if you were able to pull out the pistols, you know you can't shoot at the law. If you did the boys there will blast you to kingdom come.'

Langan had already recognized the truth of this statement. But he also knew that the confrontation had reached an impasse. Hickey would not be able to draw first, particularly against an old man, in such a public place without creating difficulties for himself. Out of the corner of his eye he watched his son help Edmund to his feet. One of the deputies approached with a menacing grin but immediately withdrew when Jack raised himself to his full height and threw him a cold hard stare. As Edmund brushed himself down, Langan dropped his hands to his side and addressed the sheriff.

'You're right, Hickey. I know that they would shoot me, but by then I would have had the satisfaction of knowing that you were well on your way to hell. But today I've got other business to attend to. I'm not going to pull a gun on you. Just stand aside and let the three of us be about our business.'

Hickey realized that this was the closest he would get to a stand-down. He nodded.

'Had your boy there not given me his lip, I would have told him about the Indians,' he said as Langan walked past him.

'What Indians?'

Hickey then relayed the information he had been given.

'So the army want you to take a

mosey up to the far end and see if any cattle have gone missin',' he concluded. 'Then you come in and let me know about it, you hear?'

'I'll go up there tomorrow, but I can find the cavalry myself to let them know.'

'Suit yourself, Langan. I told them you were an awkward cuss. Just make sure you do it first thing tomorrow, though. If there are any renegade braves around then the sooner the army finds them the better.'

The two parties dispersed in different directions. The Langans and Edmund went straight into the livery-stable. Jack was compelled to admit that he had not ridden a horse for any great distance in his life before and it was decided that he and his father would ride out in the buggy whilst Edmund accompanied them on the spare mount. The lawmen proceeded down the street to the saloon to regale Patton and any one else who would listen with the story of how they had captured the truculent miner and administered their own justice.

'Hell, Patton,' exclaimed Hickey, 'the boys did a real good job up there.'

A small awkward smile came to the lips of the saloon-owner but it came alone. It was not accompanied by enthusiasm or any further expression of gratitude. Hickey felt compelled to elaborate. He grabbed Patton's wrist and tugged him roughly towards him.

'So we are expecting a few extra dollars. Just to help Peter get his head better.'

Patton jerked himself free and leaned over the bar.

'Don't you think you get enough from me?' he whispered. 'I give you money every week and you are in here every night getting all your liquor on the house. I can't afford to give you any more.'

The sheriff reached over the bar and seized the lapels of Patton's waistcoat to allow him to haul the objector half-way over the bar. A silence fell over the saloon and the other patrons all pretended to be engaged in any activity other than watching this confrontation. With the force of a growing impatience, the sheriff freed one of his hands and slapped Patton on the side of his head.

'We have had this little parley before, Patton. If you don't want to end up just like Mitchell, you will keep the boys and me sweet. You understand?'

In a resigned voice, Patton indicated that he fully understood. He knew that Hickey wasn't bluffing. The four avengers then started on the bottle of whisky that Patton had been directed to fetch. Had they returned to the jailhouse, however, they would only have heard Mitchell emit a low doleful groan before expelling his last breath.

'So who was the stranger with Langan?' asked the sheriff as he refilled the glasses. Collectively the brothers were compelled to admit their ignorance. Billy Bob's laughter immediately subsided. He grabbed Peter. 'You don't tell me that you don't know when I ask you a question,' he shrieked. 'You get down that street and put some questions around till you find out. Then you come and tell me.'

'But Billy Bob, we were going to get a drink,' argued Peter.

The sheriff gave expression to his irritation by aiming a boot at his backside.

'You'll get a drink when I tell you you can,' he screamed. 'Now get going.'

It was an angry, humiliated, short-tempered deputy who walked into the Metropole and approached Milo.

'You had a guest last night? A stranger to these parts?'

'Yep, sure did. Came off the after-noon train. Checked out not that long ago.'

Peter walked around the reception desk and pushed Milo hard enough to send him sprawling to the floor. He lifted him up and thrust his face directly into the clerk's.

'When you have someone staying with you whom you don't recognize, you come and tell the sheriff,' he screamed. 'Do you understand?'

'Yes, Deputy. I sure do. Sure sorry about that oversight, sir,' quivered Milo.

'OK. What was this stranger called?'

'Langan.'

Hickey's face turned puce as he reached out to grab the unfortunate informer.

'Not him you fool,' he shouted. 'He ain't a stranger.'

Milo realized the source of the confusion and raised his arms to protect himself against any blows that the deputy's impatience might propel before he explained.

'I don't mean Pat Langan. I mean Jack, Jack Langan, his son. He's come from back East. Sure, he's a real live lawyer, imagine that.'

The deputy sought reassurance that he had heard correctly.

'His son?'

'Yeah, and there's more. I overheard old man Langan say that he is going to change his will to leave the whole of Far Fields to him. That's pretty bad news for Rebecca Langan, I'd say.'

Hickey released him this time. He fumed and walked out of the hotel as though he were in a trance. Milo sat down and wiped his forehead. He wondered whether he had revealed that opinion in an attempt to ingratiate himself with the deputy or whether it was simply self-preservation at work.

5

The buggy turned north and left town by the river road. They didn't look back but Jack could not prevent himself from raising the matter of the confrontation that he had just witnessed.

'Doesn't appear to be a lot of love lost between you and the sheriff back there.'

'No. I suppose there ain't. We were kind of friendly at one time but he's got a soft spot for Rebecca and he knows that I know.' Then the old man pulled a grin over his face. 'Used to keep hoping that one day I'd find them in our bed together. I could have plugged him then and no judge would have put a rope around my neck.'

Just before the army camp, Langan swung to the right and after a couple of miles crossed a wooden slatted bridge. At the other end he pulled on the reins to bring the horse to a halt.

'Well Jack,' he announced, 'this is the start of Far Fields. Two days' ride will take you to the other end.'

Under that cloudless sky, Jack surveyed the vast open stretch of grassland. In the distance a range of mountains shimmered in the haze.

'Impressive.'

'Certainly should be. Biggest ranch in the whole of this here territory, and prime grazing-land too. Edmund back there does a real good job managing the whole caboodle for me.'

Jack turned around and watched Edmund also bring his mount to a halt. Since they had left town Edmund had kept pace with the buggy but never approached nor overtook it.

'So has Edmund been with you for a while?'

'Certainly has. But now he's not just my right-hand man. He's a very good friend as well. When you take over here, look out for him and his family. His wife, Maisie, keeps house for me.'

'Pat, I told you I don't want the ranch. I'm a lawyer. You will have to find somebody else to give it to.'

'I don't have anyone else. You are my only kin. The only one.'

'Listen to me, please. I work at a desk or in a court. That's what I've done all my adult life, that's what I know about. Not herding steers or calving pregnant cows.'

The old man just smiled. 'Let's wait and see what you think after a couple of days out here in the fresh air,' he said softly. 'Get the city out of your lungs. It sure changed the way that I looked at the world.'

The ranch house was a large two-storey white painted timber building at the end of a sweeping tree-lined drive. A veranda ran around the front and a couple of rocking-chairs were strategically placed in front of the open oak door. They entered a sparsely furnished vestibule which had colourful rugs scattered on the polished floor-boards. Jack looked up the staircase, guarded by finely carved banisters, which turned on itself at the mezzanine.

'We're back,' Pat shouted. 'You there, Maisie?'

A short, smiling woman wearing a red-spotted bandana came out. Wiping her hands on her apron, she greeted Pat.

'So, Mr Langan, is this fine gentleman the son who has stopped you talking about anything else for the past month?'

'He certainly is. And I have just been telling him how welcome he is.'

Maisie had prepared supper for their return and they ate heartily. The fresh air and the ride out to the ranch house had certainly given Jack an appetite.

But he did not sleep well. After tossing and turning, he got up and poured himself a whiskey from the bottle that his father had left in his room. He took the second drink and the bottle out on to the porch and sat in the rocking-chair until the first rays of sunlight illuminated the bit of distant sky that was wedged tightly against the horizon. He returned to bed but rose only an hour later.

Maisie had laid a breakfast table, but Pat was already about to depart.

'Mornin', Jack. I would have shouted you to join me for breakfast but I know you city slickers like to sleep for a good part of the day. We are just settin' out to count the cattle at the top plain. It'll be a half-day's ride, so I guessed you would be just as happy waiting back here. If you want, you could take the buggy and drive the track down to the river. It's pretty country. Well worth seeing.'

'I'm sure it is. I might just do that. What about those Indians, though?'

'They are just renegade braves,' the old man replied in a confident voice. 'They don't mean any harm. They don't attack white men any more. They learned the hard way the consequences of doing that. They're just exploring the world outside the reservation.'

At that point Edmund entered.

'Ready now, Mr Langan,' he interrupted.

'Good, Edmund, thanks. Who is coming with us?'

'Cato and McLeish. Should we take some more of the men?'

'No, four of us are enough to count cattle and that's all we'll be doing. Just been telling Jack that the Indians don't pose any threat.'

6

Peter Hickey was out of breath when he ran into the Silver Dollar. He saw the barman refilling the glasses of the sheriff and the other deputies at the far end of the bar.

'Billy Bob, I think you should come outside to hear what I got to say,' he panted.

'Well, hell, Peter, Mr Patton here has just poured us a drink. Can't it wait?'

'I don't think you would want it to wait.'

Billy Bob lifted the glass to his mouth and swallowed the amber liquid in one gulp. He grimaced and shook his head.

'This better be good now, Peter, you hear,' he exclaimed. 'I'm not at all partial to have my drinking interrupted.'

Peter did not respond but turned and walked towards the door. The sheriff followed and the other deputies looked askance at each other, wondering what could possibly be sufficiently important and secret for Peter to call him out like that. Outside, on the boardwalk, the deputy leaned in towards his boss.

'It's his son. It's the boy that old man Langan left back East,' he whispered.

'Well, well, that sure is interesting. If he is the same troublemaking type as his father, we are going to have to keep a close eye on him too.'

'Billy Bob, that's not all. Langan's going to cut his wife out of things and pass the ranch over to him.'

The sheriff's eyes widened.

'How do you know that?' he enquired.

Peter started to recount his conversation with Milo but before he had finished the sheriff was walking over to the jailhouse. Billy Bob let out a long sigh of exasperation and thought that his day was rapidly deteriorating when he saw through the bars Mitchell's corpse slumped on the ground.

The sheriff's horse was tethered at the back of the jailhouse and he was able to ride out of town without any explanation. He followed the old mining-track that curled around the side of the hills. After two hours or so he saw the buggy and single rider far below. He guided his horse into the trees until he was sure that he wouldn't be seen, then took the track that zigzagged in its descent on to another part of Far Fields. The fine newly built house was reached by a drive with tended lawns on either side.

Maria had spotted his approach from an upstairs window. As soon as she had advised her employer she opened the door to await his arrival.

'Mrs Langan, is she at home?' the sheriff snapped as he dismounted.

'Yes, Sheriff, she says to bring you straight in.'

The sheriff was directed through the open doors and into a large ornately decorated room.

'Can I get you a beverage of some

sort?' Maria asked.

'Coffee'll do just fine.'

She was just about to invite him to take a seat when they heard the door open.

'That's OK, Maria, I'll attend to the sheriff.'

The tall woman with the long blond hair, pale skin and refined features smiled at Hickey, who jumped to his feet and snatched his hat off his head. As Maria retreated, Hickey stuttered:

'Mrs Langan, you sure are looking wonderful today. I mean, that's to say, you always look a treat. So you sure do, ma'am.' The click of the door closing gave him the reassurance that he was seeking and he stepped towards her to hold her hand. 'Rebecca,' he said, 'you know that I always make such a darn mess of things when you are around. You leave me tongue-tied. I just can't speak proper because you are so darn beautiful.'

'Billy Bob, I am a married woman. And you are a married man. I will thank you not to forget that, sir.'

'But you ain't married any more, are you. Not really, married. I mean, you don't live in his house any more.'

'No, but I still live on the ranch. And besides, you are still with Kate.'

The mention of his wife's name made him stop momentarily. He shifted uncomfortably from one foot to another before regaining some composure. Then he approached and seized both of her wrists to pull her closer towards him. When he released her, it was to stroke the soft skin of her cheeks. A sense of desire was all-consuming and he could feel the back of his throat go dry. He desperately wanted to kiss her, to let her know that she was his. She turned her face away as he spoke.

'Oh, come on Rebecca. You know that I have had a soft spot for you for ages. You can't deny that you don't feel a little bit of the same for me. I have seen you looking at me and I can read a woman's look. You know that I would leave my wife and run away with you.

You just have to say the word. An' it don't matter to me none, if you didn't have a blade of grass to your name.'

She looked at him quizzically. 'What do you mean?' she asked. 'That's a mighty strange thing to be saying, Billy Bob.'

'It's why I came here today. I have news for you. Langan's son is in town.'

She was unsure she had heard correctly.

'Jack?' she asked.

'Yeah, I think that's his name. Do you know him?'

'Pat used to speak about him. But I have never met him before. He must be . . . what, in his forties by now?'

'I reckon that could be right,' the sheriff agreed. 'Seems he's some sort of fancy lawyer, back East. But the reason he's here is that Langan is going to give him the ranch when he dies. So I guess that there would be no place for you, no more.'

Rebecca gasped, her face appearing even paler than before and the corner of her eye becoming moist with the beginning of a tear.

'He wouldn't do that,' she stuttered. 'I haven't done anything to him. I loved him. How could he take everything away from me, like that? Even the roof over my head.'

Hickey shrugged his shoulders.

'I'm only telling you what was overheard. Folk seemed pretty certain that was what he said.'

'But we built up this ranch together. I worked as hard as he did for it. That's got to count for something.'

'Not if your husband changes the will. His son will just toss you out or sell the ranch. But that don't matter none to me. I would still look after you, Rebecca.'

She had started to weep but as she listened to Hickey she wiped her tears away.

'Don't be so bloody stupid,' she snapped. 'I'm not interested in being the woman who shacks up with the town's sheriff. Far Fields is where I belong and I ain't about to give it up.'

The scorn and derision in her voice pierced him like two arrows, but he was determined that the wounds would remain invisible. He wanted her to see only his strength.

'Sure, I understand that, Rebecca, and maybe I can help you,' he said.

'You fool, no one can help me. I've got to go and see Pat and try to make him see sense. We had a good marriage at one time. He must still feel something for me, surely?'

In spite of the rhetorical nature of the question, it was addressed by Hickey.

'I can't rightly answer that, Rebecca. Folk seemed to think that his mind was made up and you know as well as I do, he's a stubborn cuss. But I don't want you to worry your pretty little head about this. I can sort it, if you want me to.'

'You? Sort it? How could you do that?'

'Best you ain't aware of that, Rebecca.'

'What do you mean?'

Before he could respond, Maria returned with an ornate silver tray. She laid it down on the small table and began to pour the coffee into two small cups. As she did, she listened to the sheriff's voice boom.

'It don't matter too much what I mean. If you want me to fix it then that's what I'll do. We're agreed?'

The rising intonation indicated a question but he left no space for an answer. Instead the sheriff picked up his hat to brush off a breeze of dust.

'I better pass on the coffee,' he concluded. 'I should be going but I promise you, I'll do what it takes. I'll be seeing you, sometime real soon.'

Maria's eyes were cast downwards, pretending she hadn't listened.

7

As soon as he was outside the house, Hickey mounted his horse and rode hard to town. He was pleased to see the town's carpenter and his mate removing the lifeless body from the jailhouse. When these makers of coffins were gone, he shouted out the names of each of his deputies. They looked over to see the sheriff beckoning them into a huddle over his desk. In a quiet furtive voice, he gave his orders.

'We got an important job to do. Peter, I want you to go over to the livery and get four fresh horses. Make sure that they've been fed and watered. John, I want blankets and torches. We are going to be riding through the night tonight.'

'Where are we going?' enquired John.

'You'll find out soon enough. For now just do as you're told.'

61

As Peter and John fetched their boss's requirements, Hickey turned to Little Bob.

'You remember those redskins that we whacked last fall?' he enquired.

'Yeah, sure do.'

'What did you do with their feathers and buckskins?'

'I hid them, Sheriff. Just like you told me,' a puzzled deputy responded. 'Remember? You told me to wrap them up and put them in that old wooden trunk in the cellar.'

As Little Bob pulled open the trap-door at the back of the jailhouse to retrieve them, Hickey walked out, took a deep breath of the fresh air and looked into the sky of the darkening day. Then the sheriff ambled over to the saloon and shouted for a bottle of whiskey. It was clear to Patton as the bottle was uncorked that there would be little chance of receiving any recompense for it. Hickey dismissed the offer of the glass that was being set down for him, took two large gulps, replaced the cork and walked back out of the saloon, carrying the bottle with him.

When they all converged again on the jailhouse, night had a firm grip on the sky above. They rode for most of that night and just before dawn they reached the opening to Blackies Canyon. Hickey scrambled up the rocky outcrop and surveyed the area with his telescope. His accomplices were crouched down around him awaiting directions.

'Right. Listen up. Langan and his boys will come past the canyon pretty soon after daybreak. I don't want them getting too close so we'll hit them when they are about two hundred yards away. You're the best shot, Peter, so I want you to concentrate on Langan. Make sure you finish him off.'

'Hell, Sheriff, this don't feel none too good. It's like cold-blooded murder. Ain't we better than that?' complained John.

Billy Bob walked towards his brother. He threw an arm around John's shoulder and pulled him closer.

'You heard what he called us back at town,' he said. "Ignorant in-breeds'. That's an insult to our daddy. I ain't about to let him get away with that. He thinks he can't be touched. We got to do it. Ain't got no choice.'

The deputies' murmurings acknowledged their understanding. The sheriff continued by looking at John and pointing to a ridge behind them.

'But if you feel queasy about it, I got another job for you. I want you and Little Bob to get changed into them Indian clothes and get up there. Make sure that you are seen as soon as we start firing. We'll keep them pinned down long enough for you to run the ridge.'

John's nod disguised his reluctance and doubts.

'Don't you want us shooting as well?' asked Little Bob.

'No, I need to convince folks that it was the Indians who ambushed him. We need some witnesses to get back.'

The morning sun rose and beat down

on the ambushers for several hours before their quarry rode into their sight. The sheriff saw them first and alerted the rest of his party with a wave.

'Don't go making any mistakes now,' he whispered. 'Nice an' easy as you squeeze that trigger.'

'*Pitchouw! pitchouw!*' The two cracks resonated with loud echoes as Edmund watched his boss fall from his horse. He was reaching for his own rifle, uselessly trapped in the leathers that held it tight against his saddle when he felt a thud to his head. Suddenly he was swimming through warm water into a comfortable oblivion.

The other two riders managed to dismount and cover themselves in a ditch which ran along the pass at that point of the track. Their pistols were drawn but the rifles had disappeared with the fleeing horses.

'Who is it?' screamed Cato.

'Look up there!' responded McLeish.

The drover had just put his head over the rim of the ditch to see the two figures dressed in buckskins and feathers sprint above them when a hail of bullets whistled into the dust, spreading a cloud through the air. McLeish ducked down and looked at his companion.

'The boss said they weren't on the warpath,' he gasped.

'Yeah, well, he got that wrong and paid for it. Edmund's a goner too.'

As the gunfire was exchanged, the impostors were taken aback by the newcomers to the scene. Little Bob was the first to spot the five ponies standing at a ledge on the other side of the canyon. For several hours the braves had watched the paleskins hide themselves and had wondered about their intent. When the sheriff caught sight of his deputy's frenetic waving, his jaw dropped.

'Jesus!' he shouted. 'It's the real Indians. Let's get out of here.'

As the lawmen ran for their horses, Cato and McLeish also noticed the braves.

'Look! More of them. If we don't vamoose they will cut us off from behind,' yelled Cato. They rolled out of the far side of the ditch and scrambled down the escarpment until they reached the sanctuary of the woods, but did not stop running. When the two parties had dispersed in different directions the Indians ventured into the mouth of the canyon. Without words, Hayin gestured to his braves to check the bodies lying on the ground.

'This one is dead,' said the brave hovering over Langan.

Hayin questioned the group congregated around the other body.

'The buffalo?'

'He still lives.'

'We must take him with us. We may need him to tell the truth about this day.'

The Indians started to construct a makeshift sledge from branches of nearby trees. As they were laying Edmund upon it one of them looked to his leader. 'Hayin, why did the white men dress as Indian brothers?' he asked.

'I have told you before, Running Wolf. The white man's world is one of deceit and lies. If they cannot find trust amongst themselves, how do they expect us to accept their promises about the reservations?'

8

When their lungs reached bursting point and when they could run no more Cato and McLeish walked as fast as the throbbing soles of their feet would allow for most of the rest of that day. The blisters burned and the muscles in their legs ached with every step. At first, the sight of blue uniforms riding towards them was doubted as a mirage but they screamed with joy when the troop reached them. They were helped on to horses and taken back to the camp beside the river where they gave a full account of their experience. When they had finished relating their tale, Lieutenant Nichol spoke.

'Do you want us to find you some blankets and a spot in one of the tents?' he asked. 'It's almost dark, now.'

Cato declined on behalf of both of them.

'Thanks, Lieutenant. But both Mr Langan and Edmund have folk waiting for them back at the ranch house. I guess that it's better they know tonight and get on with their grieving rather than worrying.'

'I understand. I'll get you some fresh horses and set you on your way. We'll go up to the canyon at first light and see if we can pick up any trails. You can tell their folks that we'll bring the bodies down as well.'

Maisie had not gone to bed but instead had sat up nursing her worry in front of the fire. She wondered why the party was taking so long to return, but she knew immediately that something not good had happened when she opened the door and saw only the two cowboys. They rejected her enquiries and insisted that they speak first to Mr Langan. When she showed them into the parlour he was sitting with a whiskey in his hand. Maisie remained, wringing her hands in an imaginary washing gesture, and no one suggested she should leave. When Cato and McLeish had finished telling their story for a second time, Maisie let out a shrieking wail and ran out of the room.

Cato caught Langan's glance.

'I'm really sorry, Mr Langan. Your father was a good man and a good rancher. He was certainly the best boss that I have ever worked for. Looked after his men real well, so he did.'

Langan's head dropped in an appreciative nod.

'There was nothin' we could do,' McLeish added. 'There was just too many of them Indians and they all had Winchesters.'

'I'm sure you did everything that you could in the circumstances. I'm learning the ways of the West pretty quickly now.'

'What you going to do now, Mr Langan. I mean about the ranch and all. You going back East?'

Langan looked at the two tired and frightened figures in front of him.

'Yes, I suppose so,' he replied. 'But

not right now. When the army brings the bodies back there'll be a couple of funerals that I want to go to. It seems really strange that it was only yesterday that I met the father that you describe. But I'm glad that I did meet him, really glad. And I want to thank you men for coming straight over to tell us.'

The survivors of that day moved uneasily from foot to foot, looking at each other, completely at a loss as to how they were going to extricate themselves from the awkward silence that followed. It was left to Langan to salvage the moment. He walked over to them with his hand outstretched. Both of them accepted the gesture.

'You have had a hard day,' he said. 'You should get over to the bunkhouse and try to get some shut-eye now.'

The invitation only required to be made once. They shuffled out of the room, hearing Maisie's rhythmic sobbing as they went through the lobby and let themselves out of the front door. Langan refreshed his glass and fell asleep in the armchair. In the morning he spotted Cato walking across the yard and asked him to harness up a buggy. The cowboy said he would.

'You going somewhere, Mr Langan?' he enquired.

'Yes. It seems the right thing to do to go across to tell Mrs Langan the news.'

'We were wondering about that, last night. You want me to drive you over there?'

'No, I reckon that I can just about manage that. Just tell me whereabouts her house is and I'll try not to get lost.'

Cato gave detailed directions and Langan pulled up outside his destination a short time later. He told Maria who he was and was shown into the drawing-room but remained standing. In a few minutes a tall, blonde woman entered. He was initially taken aback that she seemed to be about the same age as himself but then other thoughts took over. He had heard the word 'stunning' used to describe beautiful women before but this was the first time in his life that his breath had been ripped out of his throat and that his heart-beat had quickened with excitement. He tried to compose himself but could only stutter.

'Mrs Langan. I'm sorry, ma'am, to call on you unexpectedly like this.'

'Not at all, Jack. Don't be silly. I heard that you were visiting Pat and I'm delighted to get a chance to meet you. Pat used to speak about you all the time. I thought, though, that he would come with you.'

'That's just it, Mrs. Langan. That's why I'm here — '

'Rebecca, please call me Rebecca,' she interrupted.

'OK, Rebecca,' he corrected. 'But I'm afraid that I am coming with some bad news about Pat — '

Her lip quivered and she broke in before he could conclude.

'Bad news? What's the old fool been up to this time? Has he fallen off a horse again? He's too old to be doing the things that he does. I used to tell him that all the time.'

She spoke rapidly, her voice getting higher and higher as though she was trying to prevent Langan from delivering the news. Eventually she paused for breath.

'No, ma'am,' Langan said softly, 'I'm afraid that he and Edmund were killed by Indians yesterday. The army has gone up today to retrieve the bodies.'

'Oh, my God!' She sat down and let her head drop into her hands. Langan came up to her and put his arm around her shoulder. From that proximity, he could smell the heady scent of her perfume and his arm tightened just the smallest amount. She looked up and forced a smile on to her lips before speaking again.

'Thank you, Jack. Thank you for coming here to tell me. It couldn't have been easy, but Pat always said that you were a good son. You will guess from the fact that we lived apart that things between me and your father weren't easy. But he was the only man that I ever loved. I need you to know that.'

Langan nodded. 'Sure. I know it.'

She was crying as she continued and the words were distilled through sobs.

'When we first met, he could do anything. He was the smartest, strongest, quickest man around these parts. We built up the ranch together out of dirt and rocks. Then he got old and changed.'

'Changed?' asked Langan.

'He used to imagine that I was seeing other men. But he never had any cause to think that. I always loved him. I spoke to Doc Morrison about it once and he says that the mind can play funny tricks as a man gets older.'

She was staring into Langan's eyes as she continued:

'I used to just wish and wish that he had stayed the age he was when we met. He was such a handsome man then.' Langan blushed as she added: 'And you've picked up his looks.'

They spoke at length about Pat

Langan, each contributing their own memories to the discussion. Rebecca told how he had swept her off his feet when she was still a young girl and how despite parental opposition she had run away with him. Jack related his stories of his father coming home from the docks and telling him about his vision for a better future.

'He was always a dreamer, or at least that was what my mother said. And by the looks of things he made these dreams come true. At least, for himself he did.'

Rebecca shuffled awkwardly.

'Jack, I can't pretend that I didn't hear that Pat intended to change his will and pass Far Fields on to you. But this ranch has been my home for a long time. I helped build it up. I broke in the horses, mended fences. I have put my whole life into this place. I have nowhere else to go.'

'You don't need to worry,' Langan interupted. 'I'm not about to stake any claim. You are right. Pat was keen on my taking over, even had hoped that he could show me around Far Fields. But I'm a lawyer. It's in a courtroom that I feel comfortable, not out on a prairie trying to round up steers.'

A smile of relief embellished her red lips.

'But you don't have to go straight away, do you? Surely you will stay for the funeral, at least?'

'Of course. After all, Pat went out of his way to make his peace with me.'

'He'd be really pleased to know that you feel that way. I know that you were important to him. Maybe I could take you on that trip around the ranch. Show you Far Fields. Besides his boy making good, it was the one thing of which he was real proud. I think that he would want you to see it before you went home.'

Jack looked into the deep blue of her eyes and felt a wave of excitement wash over him.

'I'd like that a lot,' he replied.

They were smiling at each other

when they heard a knock at the door of the room. Maria entered and tentatively enquired whether the gentleman visitor would be staying for lunch. Langan jumped up and pulled out a full Hunter from his waistcoat pocket.

'I'm sorry. I hadn't realized the time.'

'Don't apologize. I have enjoyed your company and I am grateful that you came out to see me personally. In spite of the news that you brought. So are you going to stay and eat?'

'No, Rebecca. I want to be at Pat's house when they bring the bodies back.'

Rebecca indicated that she understood. As she stood with him on the porch waiting for the buggy to be brought around, she kissed him gently on both cheeks. Then she took hold of his hands in hers.

'You know, it's really strange,' she whispered. 'We have never met before today but I haven't felt so good talking about Pat for a long time. I'm really glad you will be there at the funeral.'

'It's been good for me too, Rebecca,' he replied.

As he drove away, he was unaware that from the small wooded copse above the house Hickey's telescope was trained upon him.

9

It was not until the following day that the expected visit from Lieutenant Nichol occurred. Langan greeted the officer and showed him into a sitting-room. He shut the door as Maisie hovered in the hall, nursing her anguished grief.

'We found the body of your father, Mr Langan. Exactly where the men said it would be. We've taken it to the undertaker's and he is awaiting your instructions regarding a coffin and burial. My condolences, Mr Langan. I am sorry for your loss.'

Jack's nod and smile of appreciation indicated acceptance of the sympathy.

'What about Edmund's body? Did you pick that up as well?'

'No, sir. There was absolutely no sign of any other body. We scoured the area just in case he had been injured, but we found nothing. Sure is mighty strange.'

'Would the Indians have taken the body?'

'Why would they? A body is only going to tie up a horse that could be used for other things and if they wanted some memento of their kill, they know how to separate the flesh from a man's skull.'

Langan gulped. 'Was my father . . . mutilated?' he stuttered. 'I mean, did they scalp him?'

'No sir. I can assure you that the body wasn't defiled in any way. He looked as peaceful as he could in the circumstances.'

The officer let his reassurance find a complete rest before he continued.

'We'll continue looking for the body of his foreman.'

'Mr Clay, Edmund Clay,' specified Langan out of a sense of respect.

'Yes sir, of course. We'll continue to search for Mr Clay's body.'

'And the Indians . . . ?'

Nichol anticipated the rest of the question.

'Not a trace of them. No tracks, no signs, nothing at all. It's as though they vanished off the face of the earth. This is their country, though, and they know it far better than any white man. After all, they were here centuries before us.'

Jack understood that Nichol was describing the futility of his task but thanked him for returning the body. Later that day, with a fevered anticipation, he drove out to see Rebecca. She welcomed him into the house, this time they hugged and he was allowed to feel the warmth of her body and smell the scent of femininity. He fancied that he might have lingered consuming the fragrance just a little bit longer than propriety would have deemed appropriate but she seemed to raise no objection. He related the news that the lieutenant had delivered and together they discussed the arrangements for the funeral of Pat Langan. As they were talking, he noticed through the window two large trunks and some items of furniture being loaded on to a wagon.

'You're not figuring on leaving are you?' he asked.

At first his question bewildered her and then she saw the scene that had precipitated it.

'Oh no. Not at all. Far Fields is almost as important to me as it was to Pat. I came here as a young girl. I've spent all my adult life on this ranch and seen it grow and grow to what it is today. Got my hands dirty on it too. A big part of me is in Far Fields, Jack. And since you told me that you won't be contesting ownership I thought that I should move back into the ranch house. Kinda fitting, I thought. You don't mind, do you? It won't put you off staying, will it? I mean, it's a big house, there's plenty of room for both of us. And besides, it would be comforting being around someone while the arrangements for the funeral are going on.'

Jack assured her that he would not be

inconvenienced in any way by her moving into the ranch house and they proceeded to talk about the funeral. Rebecca suggested that they have the grave dug on the small green hill that overlooked the big pool in the river and Jack told her that sounded like the sort of place of which his father would approve. She seemed pleased and excited with his approbation. She jumped up suddenly.

'Come on and I shall show it to you. It was always one of his favourite spots. I'll get a couple of horses saddled up. It will be a lot quicker than the buggy.'

'What, now?'

'Yes, of course. I want you to see it. I want us to do this together.'

'I'm afraid it's been some time since I rode a horse for any distance. Don't get much need in New York. I'm just a city slicker still, you know.'

'That's OK.' She laughed. 'It's not that far away and anyway, I'll help you. I'll pick you up if you fall off.'

The horses proceeded at a sedate

pace until they reached the top of the hillock. Then Rebecca and Jack dismounted. On the ground was a carpet of wild flowers and the cacophony of birdsong provided the background music. They walked together to the peak and as he helped her over the rocky outcrop that guarded the summit, she smiled warmly at him and continued to grip his smooth palm. She noticed how it was completely devoid of the rough callouses and cuts that she had been accustomed to seeing on the hands of both her husband and the cowboys who worked the ranch.

The panoramic view of wide, open prairies flanked by low rolling hills seemed to go on for ever. Jack sat down and stretched out under the sun. He pulled a stalk of grass out of the ground and began to chew on its end. Rebecca lay down beside him and their bodies moved closer to each other until there was hardly room for that green blade in between. He gazed at her milky white skin and was transfixed by the womanly shape of her body under her shirt. The top buttons were undone and in the gap created he could see the rounded fullness of her breasts. He felt a surge of lust, an excitement to which he had grown completely unaccustomed. It was though a stranger had just introduced himself as a forgotten friend.

'You know Rebecca, you are a mighty handsome woman. I can understand why my father was sorely taken by you.'

'Well, thank you, Jack. That's kind of you to say these words.'

'No, it's not kind at all. I really mean it. I haven't looked at a woman this way since my wife died. And it sure isn't easy that it's my father's widow.'

Her smile widened and her hand came to rest in his as she responded.

'No, I can understand that. And it would be unfair of me not to say that I don't have some similar feelings towards you.'

His lips were moving closer to hers and their gazes remained transfixed on each other. Just as he went to plant the kiss that had been consuming his intention, though, she moved to one side and his advance was transformed into an awkward adolescent lunge. He stopped himself falling on to the ground only by putting out an out-stretched arm. She leapt up and with her hands brushed the grass off her skirt.

'What are you doing?' she snapped. 'What on earth are you up to?'

The indignation in her voice tore through him as he too rose.

'I am so sorry,' he replied. 'I don't know whatever came over me. I just felt so comfortable with you and, to be honest, wanted to kiss you so much. I am sorry. It was really rude of me, ma'am. Please forgive me.'

After a moment of torturous silence, she spoke again. He tone was subdued and she took hold of his hand. That smooth hand that didn't belong to these wild parts. It was the hand of a man who had never roped a steer, broken in a horse or mended fences.

'It's OK. You're forgiven. Don't beat yourself up about it. It was only a kiss — or rather, it was only nearly a kiss.' She finished speaking by releasing a small laugh.

Through a strangling embarrassment he forced himself to join in her laugh. She moved in towards him, put her arms around his neck before burying her face in his chest.

'Oh, Jack,' she said. 'What's brought you into my life now? I really do feel for you and we get along so fine. You remind me of the way Pat used to be. Before he got old. I loved him so much then, I really did. And now you bring it all back for me.'

He said nothing. He carried on squeezing her tightly, hoping that the moment would not end by her breaking free as she continued: 'But that's just it. You are your father's son and when we are together I can't help but feel his presence as well.'

'I have got to tell you, Rebecca, that just now, just at this moment I want you so badly.'

'Don't say that, Jack. You know you don't mean it. It's been a strange time for us all. You must be confused with what's happening too.'

'I'm not confused at all. I sensed from the way you smile at me, the way you talk to me, that these feelings are not all only on my part. They were there the first time we met.'

He could feel her fingernails pressing through the cloth of his shirt and into his flesh. She looked into his eyes and resolutely held her gaze.

'Yes of course there is. But it's too complicated. We shouldn't be having these feelings. I've got to be sure that anything I feel for you is not just because you remind me so much of him. There can never be anything but friendship between us until I can see both you and your father as the young man that I married in the same room and know in my heart of hearts that it would be you that I would come to.'

'In which case, I shall just have to

settle for your friendship in the meantime.'

'I think it could be a very good friendship,' she proclaimed as she continued hugging him. Langan looked up at that moment and fancied that in the distance he caught sight of something reflecting the rays of the sun. He did not want to be distracted from the intimacy that he was now experiencing and dismissed it as some type of mirage.

When at last they remounted and made their way down off the hill, Sheriff Hickey came out from behind the rock on the adjacent rise. He rammed his telescope shut, propelled by the venom that was welling up in his throat and with his naked eye watched the two tiny figures disappear over the horizon.

About half a mile from her house Rebecca challenged her companion to a race.

'I don't think so.' Langan smiled. 'Remember, I'm still kind of rusty about riding.' But she wasn't listening. Instead, she used the reins of her mount to whip the rump of Jack's horse. The animal immediately accelerated from a canter into a gallop and as Jack's left boot jolted free from the stirrup, he was pulled over to the other side of the horse. He looked ungainly and awkward as he desperately tried to hold on to the saddle and prevent himself from falling off. After a couple of hundred yards, the mount slowed and he noticed Rebecca riding along beside him. Her playful expression was in direct contrast to the anguish painted on his face. She was laughing when she caught hold of the reins and persuaded Jack's horse to slow down to a pace that allowed him to regain his seat.

'Heh, what would your father say if he knew that his greenhorn son couldn't race a horse?'

'Maybe he'd be pretty disappointed.'

The two horses were now proceeding in a parallel trot up the drive of her house. She looked over and tossed her hair back into the wind.

'No, I don't think he'd ever be disappointed in you,' she responded. 'He was always mighty proud about what you achieved.'

They were both so engrossed in this conversation that they did not notice the sheriff standing at the side of the porch until they were almost ready to dismount. Rebecca reeled.

'Sheriff Hickey!' she exclaimed. 'My goodness, what a surprise you gave us. I didn't realize that you intended to call today.'

The sheriff merely continued to move his jaw from side to side whilst his eyes screwed up in a menacing stare. When he did open his mouth, his teeth were stained brown from the tobacco.

'No, Mrs Langan. I guess that you didn't. I know that Pat and I didn't necessarily see eye to eye all the time. But we knew each other for a few years. I just thought that I should come out to pass on my condolences about your husband.'

'That's mighty kind of you, Sheriff.' Before she could say any more though, Hickey cast his stare in the direction of Jack and interrupted with a snap.

'But maybe you are getting all the sympathy a woman could need at a time like this.'

The embarrassment as she introduced Jack caused a red glow to flush her cheeks.

'This gentleman here is Pat's son. He's helping me take care of the funeral arrangements.'

'Oh, I know all about the fancy-pants lawyer. We have met before.'

Langan now had his feet safely planted on the ground again. He approached Hickey with his palm outstretched.

'That's right, Sheriff. Although circumstances prevented us from being formally introduced then.'

Hickey disregarded the proffered handshake, turned his head to the side and spat out the small brown lump of tobacco that was occupying his mouth.

'We do things differently out here, Langan,' he said. 'I only take the hands of those I consider to be my friends. And I never have got to trust any of you folk from back East a whole lot further than I can throw that horse you just got off.'

Langan's hand dropped to his side but the sheriff persisted. 'You don't wear a gun, Langan. That ain't very clever around these parts.'

'I don't need a gun, Sheriff. I believe the law is there to give me all the protection I need.'

'As I say, we do things differently around here. Out here a man's got to look after what's rightfully his. His land, his animals.' Then he jerked his neck so that his eyes fixed on Rebecca as he continued: 'his woman.'

He was still staring lasciviously at her and his tongue licked his top lip as he continued to question Jack. 'So Langan, how long you figuring on staying in Idaho?'

The testy response from Rebecca

stunned both men.

'I'll thank you to keep a civil tongue in your head. Mr Langan's a guest of mine, Sheriff. You have no right asking him when he's going. That's his business. So if you have nothing more you wish to say to me, I want you off my land right now.'

Langan was the first to recover from the surprise. He noticed the sheriff had not moved one inch from the spot he occupied when Rebecca had started to berate him. He coughed to draw the lawman's attention back to him.

'I'll be here for the funeral and after that, well we'll have to see.'

Hickey felt a wave of fury rise up inside him, a fury that he could not tolerate. He didn't care who it was, no one had the right to speak to him in the way that Rebecca had just done. But even though the words had sprung from Rebecca's mouth, it was Langan, he felt, who had created the situation. It was his turn to flush, but with anger. This anger found expression in his voice. 'You can stay for the funeral but after that I want you on your way,' he barked viciously. 'Out of here. You hear me?'

Langan was just about to respond when he heard Rebecca say:

'I told you, Hickey. I want you off this land, now.'

'I've said what I came to say, ma'am, so I'll be going now.' As he walked away to retrieve his horse, he looked back at Jack. 'You mind what I said there. I want you gone as soon as the funeral's over or else you will regret the day you were born.'

They watched the dust cloud from the clattering hoofs of his horse rise into the air as it galloped down the drive at full speed.

'He seems mighty sore,' Langan observed. 'I knew that he wasn't that friendly with Pat any more, but I'm not sure what I have done to upset him.'

'Don't bother with him. He's just a blow-hard. C'mon inside. Let's get washed up and have something to eat.'

10

Pat Langan's funeral took place two days later. In keeping with the tradition of the time, the trip to the graveside was an all-male affair. Rebecca with Maria and Maisie Clay waited at the ranch house. Jack led the impressively large entourage of mourners, including all of the notables of the Cattlemen's Association, to his father's final resting-place. The preacher gathered them around and spoke of Pat Langan's vision of a tamed frontier and his courage in helping to realize that vision. As the assembly sang an off-key version of the twenty-third psalm, the coffin was lowered. Then each man lifted a small pile of dirt and threw it into the deep hole on that wild hillside. Jack was the first to release the earth from his hand and as the dirt hit the wooden lid, it made a slight, strange

98

scratching noise.

He made his way down the hill a little to the point where horses, buggies and wagons had been left. He stood at his own buggy and shook hands with the mourners as they arrived. The majority of them were complete strangers to him but they all seemed to have had a special relationship with his father. Two men stood back, though, awaiting the completion of this ritual. Then the first of them, a small smartly dressed man in a dark formal suit darted over and grabbed Jack's hand.

'Mr Langan. I'm Henry Woods. Your father's lawyer.'

'Yes, Mr Woods. My father mentioned you. Seems you helped him track me down after these years. I am grateful to you.'

Woods accepted this gratitude and then leaned towards Jack.

'You will also know that your father consulted me about changing the terms of his will,' he whispered timidly.

'As I explained to Pat, I'm a pencil

pusher. I wouldn't know what to do with the ranch.'

Woods smirked.

'Quite. Quite. I understand your position but you're a lawyer too, so you will be aware that should you change your mind there are good grounds to petition the federal court to have his current will revoked in your favour.'

'Yes, I know that, but it won't be necessary, Mr Woods.'

The lawyer shook Langan's hand vigorously but before releasing it, he spoke again.

'So be it then. As long as you know that if you ever need me to provide an affidavit that it was your father's intention to change the will just before he died and that that was the reason he arranged your trip out here, then I would be pleased to provide such a statement.'

As soon as he moved off the second man approached Langan. This time, Langan recognized Lieutenant Nichol and smiled as they shook hands. The lieutenant's brow was furled in creases of concern and he checked that all the other mourners had moved out of earshot before he spoke.

'Mr Langan, I would be grateful to have a few words about your father's murder.'

'Murder, Lieutenant? That's a strange word to use. I thought folks around these parts just accepted the danger from wayward Indians as part and parcel of the danger of coming out West. Like grizzlies or wolves.'

'That's just it, Mr Langan. I am not convinced that it was the Indians.'

Jack's mouth opened wide in astonishment.

'What do you mean? Cato and McLeish saw them. They plainly saw the Indians attacking them. They weren't hallucinating, you know.'

Nichol cupped Langan's elbow in his hand and steered him even further away from the men clambering into wagons or mounting their horses.

'Three things have been bothering

me these last couple of days. First of all, the missing body. Why would Indians take it? Like I said before, it just don't make any sense. Secondly, the number of Indians whom McLeish and Cato saw. We are pretty sure that there were at the most five of them who left the reservation. Yet there must have been at least two shooting, another couple on the ridge above and a group of about four or five on horseback coming around to cut Cato and McLeish off from the rear. It just don't add up.'

'Couldn't they have met up with some other renegades?'

'Oh sure, it's possible. But there have been no sightings of any other Indians in a two-hundred-mile radius. Apart from the Shoshone, the main group of Indians in these parts is the Pawnee and since the Sheepeater Wars, we moved all of the tribes on to reservations and set up camps to watch them.'

'But you said yourself that they are the masters of this country; they might have avoided detection until now.'

The cavalryman nodded his head in vigorous agreement and, sensing Langan's objections, he might have stopped the discussion at that point. But he was pressed.

'You said there were three things concerning you, lieutenant?'

'Yes sir, and for me the next one is the most suspicious of them all.'

One of the other mourners had started to approach the two men as they talked, but when he saw how easily Langan acceded to Nichol's encouragement to continue walking in the opposite direction, he backed off and allowed the discussion to continue in private.

'I had a close look at your father's body when we picked it up and was surprised to see two holes so close together.' The officer pointed on his own body to two points, one in the chest and the other just two inches lower directly over his heart. He saw Langan's quizzical look as he struggled to understand.

'That's the sort of holes that a repeating rifle would make,' he elaborated. 'A Henry or a Winchester. One man firing and then pulling the trigger again on the recoil. Ties in with what Cato told me. Two clear shots at your father and then another shot at Clay. I took the liberty of asking the doc to dig out the bullets and sure enough, he found two .44 shells.'

'I'm sorry, Lieutenant, you are losing me. What on earth does that prove?'

'It don't prove anything, I'm afraid. This is all about probability. But as far as we know the Indians have only single shotguns, trade muskets. They fire bigger, heavier shots, .52 calibre and the like but only one at a time. You don't need repeaters to hunt, they are the guns of war. Geronimo and his braves gave us a bloody nose back in 'seventy six because we didn't expect them to have Winchesters. In fact there's a place down there called Henry Hill because of the number of repeater casings we found after the battle. So when we moved them on to the reservations, we made darn sure that they exchanged all their repeaters for hunting-guns.'

Langan's face grew paler. Gradually the strength of Nichol's argument was dawning upon him but he continued to resist it.

'Couldn't this group have picked up a repeater from somewhere else? I mean, if we had to take them off the Indians they must have been able to get them in the first place.'

'As I say, Mr Langan, anything is possible. We know that there are some half-breed gunrunners that come down from Canada from time to time. And they would certainly trade repeaters. But we haven't seen any of them since we have been patrolling this part of the country and besides, our bunch of Indians don't have that much to trade with. So I got to ask myself, how these Indians came to have repeaters.'

A moment's thought prevented Jack from making an immediate reply. When he did speak, he was looking deep into the officer's face.

'That's all very interesting, lieutenant. But it's just a theory. What are you going to do with it?'

'I don't rightly know, Mr Langan. I sent a report to my major, but he's not convinced. Major Kaisen is of the old school, I'm afraid, when it comes to dealing with the Indians. He's a bit scarred from his time in the Indians Wars. He was up at Little Bighorn after Custer was massacred, clearing up the bodies. That's why I came along to the funeral because I wanted to talk to you in confidence. The army is pretty set on finding these Indians and making an example of them. I guess we are not over-keen on giving them a chance to explain themselves. It would suit our purposes down to the ground to avenge your father's death by hanging them or shooting them down. That way all the rest of them would get to hear about it and realize how dangerous the white man's world was for them. It would be a big 'stay on the reservation' notice.'

Langan had listened attentively and waited until he was sure the lieutenant had finished before replying.

'It wouldn't suit me though, Lieutenant. I am concerned with the truth and if it wasn't the Indians, then I want to find out who is responsible.'

'I'm glad you said that. There's not a lot that I can do by myself but if you went to the sheriff then he could ask some questions.'

'I'm afraid that the sheriff and my father were not on the best of terms.'

'I don't think that matters too much. All he needs to do is to tell the army that he has some doubts and the Indians Office will send in federal agents to oversee the investigation.'

The firm grip of the handshake with which Langan bade the officer goodbye expressed his gratitude for sharing these thoughts.

When he returned to the ranch house a number of the mourners were milling around. Rebecca had also come over and was consoling Maisie when he entered. She was dressed all in black with a lace veil covering her face.

As at the graveside, men approached him, wanting to press his flesh and tell him how much they admired and respected his father. His smile was sufficiently courteous to avoid offending any of them. But he wanted to be alone and when he managed that, he found an unopened bottle of whiskey. He pulled out the cork and threw it on to the floor before crushing it with his boot. He knew that he would drain the contents of the bottle before needing to replace it.

After all the mourners had departed, Jack and Rebecca were left alone. They sat down together and he handed her a glass. She accepted it before speaking.

'I'm really pleased that you were around today. It wasn't easy meeting all those folks and them all knowing that Pat and I were man and wife in name only.'

'I'm sorry that I couldn't be of more

help. I just had to clear my head for a little while.' He was still looking into her eyes when he continued: 'You look beautiful in that black dress. It makes the gold of your hair stand out.'

She smiled and moved closer. 'Black is the colour of grief but I'm grieving not just for the loss of Pat. I'm grieving for me because I'm alone now. I've got nobody whom I can grow old with, no-one whom I can share my life with.'

Jack shifted uneasily, then changed the direction of the discussion.

'Rebecca, there's something important I got to ask you.' She threw a cautious look over the couch as Jack enquired: 'Did Pat have any enemies? Was there anybody who really hated him? Anybody who might be ruthless enough to consider murder.'

His last word resonated inside her head before the vision of Hickey's face flooded her mind. She recoiled at the memory of the discussion she had had the day the sheriff rode out to tell her about Jack's presence. Then she addressed the question.

'Murder? No, I don't think so. I mean, he was a hard businessman and he could be pretty single-minded when he wanted to. Sure, there have been a few of the hands over the years that he has had to throw off the ranch. And a few of the smaller ranchers round these parts think that Pat drove the price of beef down to force them out of business. Some of them might still feel a little bit aggrieved, but that's a long way from wanting to kill him. But why are you asking? We know it was the Indians.'

Jack slowly and carefully recounted Nichol's points. When he had finished Rebecca seemed to be breathless and excited.

'No, that doesn't make sense at all,' she protested. 'It's only the Army covering themselves. After all, it was Nichol who told the sheriff the Indians posed no threat. If anything he was the one who was responsible for Pat going up to the canyon with only a few men.

The cavalry should have checked it out themselves rather than asking civilians to do their job.'

'Maybe, maybe not. I don't know. But I have got to go and speak to the sheriff. At the very least he can pass on these doubts to someone who will investigate them.'

'Don't be stupid, Jack. You know that Hickey didn't like Pat and he doesn't seem too enamoured of you either. He's not going to do anything.'

'He has a job to do and if Idaho really does want to come into the Union then the rule of law has to be upheld. He wouldn't dare just sit on this complaint. The Territory's leaders down in Boise would sack him and that would be the end of the little fiefdom that he's running up here.'

She moved away from him even further. He could not understand why she was becoming so flustered and irritated but it was naked anger that carried her next words.

'Hickey was correct. You don't have

even the beginning of an understanding of the way things work out here. Your words and rules might be OK for life back East but this is different, very different. Hickey will do just as he pleases. He's a one-man law unto himself. I'm asking you, Jack, just to let this drop. Otherwise, it could be dangerous for you.'

He stood up and walked around the room. His head was buried into his chest and she had to struggle to hear the barely audible words.

'I'm disappointed you see it that way, Rebecca. I know that you and Pat had your problems together, but I would have hoped that there might still have been enough there for you to be interested in finding out the truth about his death.'

Now she jumped up so that she could look him in the eye without straining her neck.

'You fool, you damned fool,' she shrieked through sobs. 'This has got nothing to do with me and Pat. It's about you and me. If you have any feelings for me at all you will let this all drop.'

He started to protest but she ignored him and advancing until she was only inches away, put her index finger gently over his mouth.

'Let's both get the train tomorrow,' she suggested. 'Let's get away together. I have never been to New York before but I feel that I know it from Pat's stories. I would love to see it and I would like to be with you when I do.'

He was startled by her proposal but she left him no opportunity to respond before she left. After the door was closed he could hear her moving about upstairs in the master bedroom. When he found that the whiskey was finished, he searched various cupboards until he found another bottle. With this trophy, he returned to his seat and refilled his glass. Although he pulled a blanket over his waist a couple of hours later when the chill of the night began to bite, he did not sleep. It was a full moon and a cloudless sky that night. Shafts of moonlight poured in through the window, which made him feel that he was sitting on an illuminated stage: an actor in some sort of play. He found himself in a situation that was unreal and completely divorced from his life back in New York. Rebecca's words were imprinted at the front of his mind like a giant sign but behind them he could see two visions returned from the dead. That of his wife, before her body became wasted with that awful consumption and that of his father, wore concerned and disappointed expressions. Although they seemed to be denied the facility of speech, Jack was left in no doubt about what they were asking from him.

When the first hint of the new day's light peeked through the window, he rose and proceeded to the stable. With some confidence from his previous equestrian experience, he decided that he would leave the buggy and ride one of the horses. He surveyed his choices and picked out the most docile-looking animal before fastening a saddle on to its back. He led his mount across the yard and looked up at the window of the master bedroom. The curtains were still drawn as he started his ride into town.

11

Hickey and his companions were huddled around the stove, drinking coffee when Langan crashed through the door without ceremony. They sprang to their feet and cast a gaze of collective suspicion towards him.

'Well, well, boys. It seems we have a visitor. Ain't that good of the fine gentleman to come and see rough-necks like us,' rasped Hickey before he snapped at Langan: 'I sure hope, mister, that you have come to say your farewell and that you are aiming to get that afternoon train out of here. The funeral's over, you've no more business here.'

'Actually, Sheriff, I do. And it concerns you as well,' countered Langan. The room fell silent as the deputies wondered how their leader would address this challenge. As Hickey's face contorted in his attempt to make sense of Langan's words Little Bob drew his pistol. But the sheriff pushed his arm back.

'Leave him be, Little Bob. I want to hear what Mr Langan thinks he has to say, that could possibly interest me sufficiently to let him stay one more day in Franklin.'

As the lawmen listened without interruption Jack Langan once again reiterated the lieutenant's thesis. When the lawyer had concluded, the sheriff turned his head away and spat a lump of tobacco out of his mouth. His next words, though, left Langan numbed with shock. 'You're under arrest, Langan. I'm throwing you in jail.'

After he had made sense of the sheriffs intent, the lawyer stuttered:

'You can't put me in jail. I've done nothing wrong. You are here to uphold the law, not abuse it.'

'Mister, I can do what I like. I'm the sheriff. I told you to leave straight after the funeral but you had to try and test me out. Now you are going to find out about the way of the world around these parts, the hard way,' Hickey asserted before snapping at Little Bob: 'Put him in the cell.'

Little Bob seized Langan's arm and pulled him towards him. He failed to see the fist on the other arm being guided through the air until it made contact with the deputy's chin. Peter and John had reached for the pickaxe handles even before Little Bob's frame slumped to the cold stone of the floor. The blow cracked against Langan's skull, but he still managed to aim his kick at the groin of the first approaching assailant. It was to little avail, though, for the next strike to his head rendered him unconscious.

'Heh! he had a bit of fight in him,' admired Peter before he picked up a bucket and marched to the tap on the wall. John, bent double and holding his testicles, cast a grudging nod of agreement through the wince of pain. The sheriff dragged the lawyer's body across the floor and into the cell. He was wheezing with exhaustion as he turned the key in the lock.

'He had a kick like a mule,' complained John as he tried to straighten up.

'Why didn't you just let Little Bob plug him?' asked Peter.

A disdainful look was on the sheriff's face.

'Because, you fool, every one knows that he doesn't carry any guns,' he responded. 'And if those interfering idiots down in Boise thought that we had shot an unarmed man, they would get itchy about their statehood application. That would really upset the apple-cart. We would have all sorts of fancy pants up here conducting their investigations.' His last word was spat out with venomous derision.

'So what we going to do with him now?' asked Peter as he sent a torrent of cold water over the inert body of his brother. 'Do you think Langan knew it was us who bushwhacked his old man?'

Hickey addressed the second question first.

'I don't know. He's not a fool but I think he was genuinely asking us to do something about the killing, so maybe he has got just a little bit too much belief in the law. Anyway it don't matter none, he ain't going to be too pleased when he wakes up, so we got to get rid of him now. I can't have him using that lawyer brain to be complaining about the way we run this town.'

'So what about taking him up country and shooting him. We could blame it on the Indians again,' suggested Peter.

'No!' exclaimed the sheriff. 'You heard what he said about the calibre of the guns. We don't want anybody digging a shell out of him and asking more questions.'

As he spoke he walked to the window and pulled the grimy net curtain back. He saw Langan's horse tethered directly outside. His face brightened as the idea formed in his head.

'But I know our friend ain't the greatest horseman in the world so if he went up country himself, say to Red River cliffs, and say his horse got spooked by a rattler or something, then he might get thrown over. Poor man just ain't used to riding horses through rough country like this.'

Little Bob was being helped by his brothers to lift his gigantic frame to an upright position again.

He wiped the cold water from his face.

'How we going to get him to ride up the Red River?' he asked.

The lawmen smiled at the childish naïvety of their brother and then promptly ignored him.

'Get him tied up good and tight, Peter, and make sure that his mouth is gagged,' ordered the sheriff. 'And you, John, bring his horse around the back.'

John grimaced. 'Are you sure, Sheriff? I mean, wouldn't it be better if we just stuck him on the train?'

'He'll just come back to pester us if

we leave him alive. Ain't no other way around it, little brother. You man enough to do what I'm telling you?'

Reluctantly the deputy nodded and slunk outside to retrieve the mount. When the ropes that bound Langan's wrists and ankles were tied so tightly that they constricted the blood flow to his limbs, the still slumbering body was covered with an itchy horsehair blanket, carried from the cell and thrown over his own mount. The pulls, the pushes and the lift were conducted without ceremony or care. Starting to regain consciousness through being roughly manhandled, Langan imperceptibly craned his neck to listen to the sheriff utter his directions.

'So make sure, Peter, that you keep him tied up till after you throw him over the cliff. Then if he's still breathing, haul him up and throw him over again. And again, if you have to. You make sure that he's dead before you leave him. You hear me, now?'

Peter nodded as his half-brother

continued: 'Then you cut the horse loose and get straight back here. The rest of us are going to stay in town today. So if anybody asks, you were with us all day here in the jailhouse. You got that?'

Langan would remember little of that uncomfortable journey as he lapsed in and out of consciousness. He certainly failed to see the eyes that watched them from afar. But so did his captor. Six men with five horses followed their progress. Four of the Indians would take it in turn to give up their horse and run alongside the others. But in spite of this and the handicap of crossing rougher terrain, they outpaced Hickey and Langan.

Langan was still groggy when Peter dragged him down from the horse and started to heave him towards the edge of the cliff. He stumbled and fell. Peter went to pull him to his feet.

'Come on, get up. Falling to the ground ain't going to change anything. You should have thought about this when you decided not to get that train.'

Through the haze in his head, Langan imagined he saw someone standing above him on the rocky outcrop. He blinked and looked again. It was no mirage, the figure was still there. Noticing the wide stare Peter turned around to see what had caught his captive's attention. Then he dropped Langan and sprang back four paces to the horses. From his own saddlebag he pulled out his rifle and took aim at the solitary figure above him. He felt his fingers starting to squeeze the trigger but they never reached the point at which it would click and discharge its lethal message. Instead a raging burning sensation consumed the space between his shoulder blades.

The pain wrenched the rifle out of his hands but he managed to turn to see the shaft of a lance buried deep into his flesh. As he dropped to his knees he could just see the shadowy figure of another Indian approach. He was trying to focus the gaze that was becoming more and more glazed when the first Indian jumped down from the rocks and seized a tuft of his hair. With a yelp like a dog the assailant pulled Peter's head back before drawing his knife along the breadth of his victim's throat.

Langan watched with a blend of fascination and horror as the wound widened and blood spilled freely to the ground. He gasped as the lawman's eyes darted to and fro and then rolled upwards, but the gag in his mouth prevented any sound from escaping. Instead he simply averted his eyes towards the ground in the only gesture of respect to the moment of a life departing this earth that he was able to make.

When Peter slumped forward and remained motionless, Langan saw the pair of moccasins advance upon him. He determined then that if he too was about to die, he would do so while looking straight into the face of his killer. Through the hideous red and blue ochre on the advancing face, Langan stared contemptuously into the slits of hate that were eyes. He waited for the opening of his flesh but the glinting steel blade was lifted upwards, cutting through the ropes and letting his arms spring free. Then a familiar voice boomed out.

'Mr Langan. Don't worry none. You're all right now.'

He looked behind the ferocious spectre of death to see a row of Indians on horseback. Sitting behind the one in the middle and peering around was Edmund, radiating a broad grin of glistening white teeth. Langan, now believing that at least temporarily he might live, felt a tear well up at the side of one eye as he twice called out Edmund's name. He brushed the droplet away with his arm as surreptitiously as he could whilst he was trying to regain his feet. Still stiff from his recent journey, he stumbled slightly and might have fallen had Edmund not dismounted and grabbed him.

'Take it easy, Mr Langan. It sure looks as though you have had a rough time.' He pointed to the body beside them. 'We have been trailing that piece of dirt for at least ten miles wondering what was under the blanket,' he explained. As he gained some measure of composure the overwhelming sense of both confusion and relief was tangible in Langan's voice.

'You are not dead. We thought that you'd been killed. What are you doing here?'

'The Indians didn't kill the boss, but they know they have been blamed for it. They picked me up and wiped my bruises after the ambush. Now they are trying to find out who did it so that I can tell the army.'

'Yeah, I know it wasn't the Indians. That's why I went to see the sheriff today.'

Edmund's teeth were grinding when he replied: 'When the Indians told me it was paleskins dressed up, I always felt in my gut that it was Hickey and his brothers. They bear real bad grudges.'

'But we have got no evidence,' protested the lawyer. 'I doubt if anyone saw me going into the jailhouse and if they did would they really speak out against Hickey? It wouldn't stand up in court.'

'Mr Langan, I've never harboured any notion that this would be going to court. One of them's already dead. That only leaves three more of the scum. They have to come out of the jailhouse sometime. I just need surprise and a little bit of luck on my side and my old blunderbuss will even things up.'

The frustration in Langan's voice caused him to snap.

'No, Edmund. That's exactly what we are not going to do. Too many murders. You have to allow the law to sort things out, believe me. You can't bring yourself down to their level. And besides how would that help your friends here? The army would not only continue to hunt them down, but they would come after us as well for shooting the sheriff.'

'The white man has the eyes of the hawk. You must follow him, Buffalo.'

Taken aback by the use of English, Langan switched his gaze to the old man on the horse. He noticed for the first time that unlike his companions he was wearing a full head-dress of eagles' feathers. It was left to Edmund to effect the introduction.

'Mr Langan, this is Hayin. He is the medicine man of the tribe. He's sort of in charge of these Indians. He was sent by the tribe to bring them home. The braves were trying to find new hunting-grounds. Now they know there aren't any, they just want to return to their village. But first they have to clear themselves of killing your father.'

Hayin interrupted to elaborate.

'We know that the horse-soldiers are hunting us because they think that it was us who killed the old man. They can't find us, though. We can become rocks, grass and trees. But we cannot hide for ever. We have to be lucky every day and they only have to be lucky once by coming across the trail that we forgot to brush away. You and the Buffalo must go and convince them of our innocence.'

Langan gave a deferential nod that indicated he understood Hayin's position.

'I know that you didn't kill my father,' he said. 'I knew it before I saw Edmund today, but there are certain people who don't want to be told that. I'll make sure that they find out the truth.'

'You are a wise and a good man. You will know what to do when the time comes. The Buffalo will help you. He is a good man too. But it will be in the way of which you speak, not his way.' As soon as he had finished he turned his horse away and the braves quickly followed him, leaving Langan and Edmund standing alone in a still silence. A dust cloud gathered up behind the galloping animals and when it had settled the Indians had disappeared.

Edmund jumped on to the deputy's horse and crossed over to the small copse behind them where Langan's mount was now grazing, to retrieve it. When he returned Jack was bent double over a pool of vomit several feet away from the lawman's body.

'When did they do that? I didn't see it.' He gasped and then explained. 'The skin on his head has been cut off.'

Edmund merely shrugged.

Langan wiped away the tangible signs of his disgust and shook his head. Eventually he enquired of his companion:

'What we going to do with this piece of scum? The body, I mean.'

'We have to bury him. If we leave him the birds will pick the flesh right off the bone.'

Langan looked skywards and saw two vultures gliding in circles.

'Only two of them now,' explained Edmund. 'But in five minutes there'll be ten and then twenty. We only need to ride a few yards and they would swoop.

His eyes would be out before we could turn around.'

'We haven't got any shovels.'

Edmunds dismissed Langan's complaint with scorn in his voice. For three hours in the blazing sun, the two men shifted earth and rocks using their bare hands, flat stones and pieces of wind-felled branches. When they had constructed a shallow grave they lifted the mutilated body into it and covered it up.

'Well, someone else can pass judgement on his soul now,' observed Edmund.

Jack smiled. 'Hayin was right. You are a good man. But why did they call you 'Buffalo'?'

The perpetual grin turned into a laugh as Edmund tugged at the short curly hair on his head.

'They saw quite a few black men during the Indian wars and they called us all buffalo soldiers. I think it's because this reminds them of buffalo fur.'

As Jack was hauling his sore and sorry body into the saddle, he looked into Edmund's eyes and suggested that they go straight to the army camp.

'Yes, sure, Mr Langan. If it wasn't for those Indians, I'd be a dead man by now.'

12

About fifty yards down the road from the camp, a sentry stood. He moved to block the path of the two horsemen. When they had stopped, he demanded to know their business. Langan replied, 'We need to see your commanding officer, Lieutenant Nichol. We have some really important news about the Indians you are looking for.'

'The lieutenant ain't the commanding officer of this camp no more. That's been taken over by Major Kaisen now.'

'Alright, we've got to talk to him then. But quickly, it's important.'

The soldier untied his horse from a tree and bade them follow him down the row of white canvas tents. In the centre there was a tent much larger than the rest outside which the sentry dismounted. He instructed Langan and Edmund to do likewise.

'Wait here,' he told them. 'I'll let you know whether the major can see you.'

He returned after a few moments and held open the flap of the tent to indicate that they should enter. When they did they saw a small man with a white beard and three rings of gold braid on each sleeve of his coat. Behind him stood another two officers but he pointed to seats to indicate that they should sit down. As they were doing so, he spoke.

'Gentlemen, I'm Major George H. Kaisen. I understand from the sentry that you can tell us where we can find these varmints.'

Langan immediately corrected him.

'No sir. That isn't exactly the case. But we can help you to do right. I'm Jack Langan, the son of the rancher who was killed recently up at Blackies Canyon. And this here is Edmund Clay, who was with him at the time. We've come to tell you that the Indians are not responsible for the killing. In fact they were the ones who rescued

Edmund from the bushwhackers.'

The major's face turned puce. He spun around in his chair and shouted at one of the officers behind him.

'Get Nichol. Get him here, now.'

The officer snapped his heels together, saluted and marched quickly out of the tent, as the major returned his attention to his visitors.

'Mr Langan, I don't know what's your game but you better have a good story to come in here and try to stick up for savages.'

Langan took a deep breath in an attempt to conceal the surprise he felt at this reception and started to recount systematically the story from the point when he had arrived at the sheriff's office earlier in that long day. Edmund nodded vigorously as his involvement was included in the account of events that were being laid out in front of the major. Just as it was being concluded, Nichol entered the tent and although he saluted his commanding officer he was blatantly ignored. When Langan finished, the major's face was still red with anger. He thrust a contemptuous glance into Langan's face.

'You, sir. You're some kind of expert in Indian matters are you?'

'Well, no sir. But I know what I have seen and I have Edmund here as a witness.'

The major sat silently nodding his head before he screamed at the assembled company.

'So the fine visitor from back East wants to tell us some cock-and-bull story because he doesn't like what we are doing. We have all heard about the bleeding-heart brigade, haven't we, gentlemen? They waste their energies lobbying the Indian Office to allow these savages off the reservations, to move freely through the country, looting and plundering and killing decent folk.'

The major chose not to notice his embarrassed officers casting their eyes downwards to avoid his gaze but instead stared at Langan. 'But I really thought, sir,' he continued in more moderate tones, 'that given they ambushed your father, you would not be a party to that abomination. We know that these evil savages are thieves and murderers. You are telling me that they killed and scalped a duly appointed officer of the law of this territory and you are sticking up for them in the same breath. Did this Indian-lover put you up to it?'

He stabbed his finger in the direction of Lieutenant Nichol whose face was now equally red. Nichol's mouth began to open but the major cut across to continue.

'You can't fool me. The men told me that the two of you were seen deep in cahoots at the rancher's funeral. I was just wondering what you were conspiring about. Now I know.'

Surprise and indignation initially joined forces to stifle any objection but eventually Nichol found the voice to express his protest.

'I resent that, sir. I try to do my job

as an army officer as fairly as I can and to the best of my ability. And I still believe that the evidence against the Indians being responsible is compelling.'

'Shut up, Lieutenant,' Kaisen commanded. 'You will answer me only when I speak to you.'

Langan now leaned forward and after releasing the bite that he had imposed upon his own tongue spoke softly.

'What I have told you is the absolute truth. I know that whoever killed my father it wasn't the Indians. I'm sorry about Deputy Hickey but as sure as God is my witness, I'm telling you that if the Indians hadn't come along at that moment, I wouldn't be here. And it has left a mighty sour taste in my mouth when I think about the sheriff and his brothers.'

'Mister, whatever you're chewing on I would keep that mouth shut, if I was you,' sneered the commanding officer. 'You can't go around these here parts making accusations against the sheriff and expect to stay healthy.'

'Why would I lie? Why would Edmund lie?'

'I told you why you would lie. Because you just ain't got the guts for the things that have to be done out here, to keep the territory safe for the God-fearing folk that put their lives at risk trying to earn a living. And as for your friend here, well take it from me, his kind is just plain used to lying. You want to know what I think. I think that he shit his pants when he got bushwhacked and ran off and hid out for a few days. Then you come across him when you are out riding the outback and he gives you the fairytale that you just spun.'

'That's preposterous. How dare you, sir?'

The major also jumped up and pressed his face into Langan's.

'How dare I?' he shouted. 'I'll tell you how I dare. I have been commissioned to track these red vermin down and stop their killing. That's how I dare.

And if I have to string up every last brave to ensure that not one more decent law-abiding citizen of this Territory loses his life, then so be it, sir.'

He let his voice hang on this last word in a sarcastic gesture before Langan responded.

'You will never find them. They are far too clever for white men.'

The major's lips turned upwards in a scornful grin.

'Maybe, maybe so — but we ain't using white men any more to look for them. I have a dozen Indian scouts coming down here tomorrow.'

The sharp gasp of air indicated that this development was news to Nichol. The major, however, merely gave a perfunctory nod with his head.

'Now get out of my sight,' he barked.

Langan was the first to realize the futility of further argument and led the procession out of the tent. Holding a lantern above his head, Nichol turned to face him. 'I'm sorry for what happened in there,' he said. 'But at least we know the truth, now.'

'Yeah, but what good is that to us. Or the Indians?' queried Edmund.

'We can ride out at first light and warn them. We might never be able to find them but as sure as eggs are eggs they will find us. Perhaps if they can get back to their reservation, they will find sanctuary,' offered Langan.

But the lieutenant was already anticipating the tactics of his superior officer.

'No, you can't go near the Indians. Warning them is precisely what the major will expect you to do. He'll be having you followed and as soon as the Indians come out of hiding to meet you, they'll be trailed. And when the troop catches up with them, they'll just be massacred. The last thing he wants is to take prisoners. Dead men won't trouble anybody by protesting their innocence.'

13

Langan and Edmund decided that it would be foolish not to accept the lieutenant's offer of a tent for the night. But both were awake long before dawn and after retrieving their mounts, rode out of the camp as soon as there was sufficient light to let them follow their route. They chose the high path, climbing over the hill, rather than the better-maintained road that stuck tightly to the riverbank. They knew that would reduce the prospects of meeting anyone else. As they reached the highest point of the track and looked backwards they both noticed that they were being trailed by two horsemen wearing the distinctive blue tunics of the US cavalry.

'Not doing too good a job at keeping out of sight,' observed Edmund.

'No,' responded Langan. 'When there's

only two of them I guess they don't want to run into the Indians any more than anyone else.'

Maisie Clay was sweeping the front porch when she looked up to see two unexpected horsemen trotting up the drive. She wiped the dust out of her eyes but when she pulled her hands away again the vision of her husband still remained.

'Lord preserve us!' she screamed at the top of her voice. Her broom was discarded as she stumbled down the steps and fell to her knees. She was still mumbling prayers as Edmund dismounted and gently lifted her up.

'It's alright, Maisie. I'm alive. I'm alive just like you. I was never killed. The Indians saved me and then they rescued Mr Langan here as well.'

At the mention of the name, she wiped tears away from her eyes and cast her glance towards the dismounting figure. Langan smiled.

'I told him you would be surprised. Is Mrs Langan about the house?'

She would have answered him, had she not heard the shout behind her.

'Jack, Jack. Oh, my God. You're back!'

Rebecca was rushing through the open door and collided into him. His arms caught her and she entwined herself around him, hugging him tightly. He wanted to kiss her passionately but he remembered the last time he had made that approach and was also aware of the two pairs of eyes focused upon them. After a few moments engaged in celebratory embrace, Langan suggested that they go inside. As soon as they crossed the portal, each of the couples went their respective ways and Langan found himself in the parlour with Rebecca pouring him a stiff drink. He quickly told her the briefest of details of the previous day and she waited until he finished before passing over the glass. He sipped the whiskey and savoured the warming feeling. It was an affirmation that he had survived his encounter with the sheriff.

As soon as he put the glass down, Rebecca started to castigate him for setting off on his expedition to confront Hickey against her advice.

'You are lucky to be alive. Didn't you realize how dangerous Hickey is? I asked you not to go. I asked you to take me to New York, instead. Didn't that mean anything to you?'

'Of course it did, Rebecca. And it was a mighty tempting offer, just forgetting everything the lieutenant told me and running away with you. But I've got to live with myself. I took the coward's way out once before in my life and I learned how hard it really is. I couldn't do it again. Please understand that.'

Her voice became softer and a solitary tear formed in the corner of her eye.

'We were so worried about you,' she said. 'I mean I was worried about you. I told you that Hickey can be a nasty piece of work. But nasty as he is I'm still shocked that he tried to kill you.

Why ever would he do such a thing?'

He looked directly at her as he explained.

'He tried to kill me because he was the one who shot Pat. I have to prove it though, in a way that will convince that fool of a major.'

The surprise registered on her face and it was a few moments before she spoke again.

'How are you going to do that?'

'I don't know yet, but when Hickey realizes that I'm not dead, he's going to get pretty jittery. So after I finish this drink and then have some food, I am going to pay him a visit. That should raise the stakes of this game a little.'

Her voice was raised again.

'What? After yesterday? You are going back there? You have lost your mind. You are mad. He will just shoot you.'

'He can't shoot me. I don't carry any guns. Even a sheriff would be hanged for shooting an unarmed man who had come to see him. Folk are worried about this application for statehood and it's even more important now to show the government that out here in Idaho, the West ain't so wild any more.'

'But he would just do the same as before, then, and try to arrange an accident for you. He's going to be pretty sore when he finds out that his brother has been killed. He'll blame you for it and whatever anyone says about those Hickey boys, they have always stood together.'

'I'm kind of hoping for that, Rebecca. 'Cos you see, I got an escort now. And if he tries anything he will have to do so in front of the US Army's finest.' He pulled back the lace curtains and pointed to a large old oak tree at the end of the drive. In arboreal shade, two soldiers rested, their horses tethered to a branch.

'Who are they? What are they doing here?' Rebecca queried and then listened as Langan explained.

'The major seems pretty keen on making an example of the Indians. That's why I got to prove that they didn't kill my father, and I don't have a lot of time to do it.'

'Why? Why have you? It's no business of yours. Just let it go. Please.'

Langan laughed.

'I'm not a complete fool,' he said. 'Hickey will not touch a hair of my head as long as he sees those soldiers there.'

'I'm not only frightened for you,' she snapped. 'I'm frightened for me as well. I don't want to lose you.' As the words dropped out of her mouth she turned around to face him and they stared into each other's eyes. Eventually she raised herself up on her toes and planted her mouth over his. His arms enveloped her and they were locked together, oblivious to the rest of the world, as time itself seemed to freeze. He had to push her away slightly to look into her eyes. His tone was stern and determined when he said:

'Rebecca, it's been a real long time since I held such an attractive woman in my arms. But right now, I have to put this whole sorry mess to rights. Not just because Pat was my father but because these Indians saved my life. I owe them an incredible debt and I wouldn't be able to live with myself if I didn't try to repay it.'

She exhaled and looked down at the floor. To herself, she acknowledged the steely resolution of his intent. Her response was spoken in a soft but determined voice that defied argument.

'All right then. If that's how you feel, why don't you go into the kitchen and get Maisie to rustle you up some breakfast and I'll saddle up two fresh horses.'

'Two?' he repeated.

'Yes,' she confirmed. 'I'm coming too.'

'But, but . . . ' he tried to interrupt, as she cut across him.

'And don't go giving me any story about it being too dangerous. You have already said that your military escort will be guaranteeing your safety. I guess that goes for mine too.'

He knew that argument would be futile.

14

The mood in the jailhouse was sombre. When Peter failed to return the previous evening Little Bob had expressed concerns, but these were perfunctorily dismissed by the sheriff.

'I'm telling you, Little Bob, he'll be all right. He's just a little late, that's all. Maybe his horse got lame or something and he's having to walk.'

When night fully cloaked the sky, however, they were all worried. The sheriff promised that if Peter had not returned after they had completed their breakfast the following morning, they would all set out to find him. Then they were distracted by a fight between some ranchers and miners in the Silver Dollar. They speedily resolved the dispute through a judicious use of the pick-handles, which involved bruising a few heads and cracking some ribs. Jess

Patton had demonstrated his gratitude by passing over to them a few beers and a bottle of whiskey. Consequently it was later in the morning than they had originally planned when they converged outside the jailhouse.

The fortuitous delay, though, allowed them to see the cavalry procession arrive in town. As they watched it approach, the sheriff recognized the gold braid of a major on the small squat man on the leading horse. He removed his hat and stepped off the boardwalk to hold the reins of the major's horse as it came to a halt.

'You the sheriff in this here town?' barked Kaisen.

'Yes sir, sure am. Sheriff Hickey. What can I do for you, Major.'

'You missing a deputy today?'

The blood drained from Hickey's face, turning him dramatically ashen.

'Yes,' he replied at last. 'We were just about to set out to find him. But how did you know that, Major?'

Kaisen ignored the question and

from the saddle continued with his enquiries.

'So when did you last see him?'

'Yesterday. We had a plumb loco greenhorn in here saying that he was going to ride up to Blackies Canyon. What with these Indians about and the fact that he didn't seem too comfortable in the saddle, we got kinda worried about him after he left. Didn't we boys?' Little Bob and John confirmed this concern by nodding their heads vehemently. 'So about an hour or so after he left, I sent Peter on out just to keep an eye on him,' the sheriff continued.

The major grunted. 'This greenhorn, was it a Jack Langan?'

'Yes, it sure was. Fancy lawyer from back East but can't even ride a horse properly and doesn't carry no armament to protect himself.'

'Sheriff, I regret to tell you that Mr Langan came to see me late last night. Apparently he came across the mutilated body of your deputy yesterday.

Scalped to the bone by those heathen renegades.'

'No!' screamed Little Bob and the sheriff and John were compelled to hold on to him and guide him into a sitting position on the boardwalk. Hickey was still trying to comfort Little Bob when he saw that the major was preparing to turn his mount.

'Wait!' he called out. 'If you are going up there we'll come with you.'

'That's not possible, Sheriff. This is a military matter now. Civil authorities have no jurisdiction over runaway Indians.' With those words and before any response could be formulated, Kaisen turned his horse, raised his left hand in the air and bade the troop to follow him at a gallop as he rode out of town.

15

After he had eaten and washed, Langan collected a pot of coffee and a pan full of eggs and ham. He placed them carefully in the back of the buggy and drove the few hundred yards to the largest tree in the drive. The soldiers immediately jumped to their feet as they saw him approach and started to untie their horses, but Langan reached them before they could mount.

'Hold up there, soldiers,' he said. 'No need to untie the animals. I ain't going anywhere. I just come up to see if you could use some coffee and chuck.'

When the soldiers saw Langan climb down with the nourishment, a broad smile spread across both faces. The aroma of the coffee and the food still hot pulled their noses into the air and their delight was obvious.

'Sure could, sir. That's mighty kind

of you, Mr Langan,' exclaimed the taller one. 'I'm Private Lyon by the way and this here is Private Silverstone.'

As Langan nodded an acknowledgement of the introductions he passed over the pot and pan. He could not prevent himself from studying their faces. They were just boys. Sixteen, seventeen at the most. The faces that were covered with the spots that one associates with the passing into manhood were seated on thin undernourished bodies. One of them sported strands of thin wispy hair on his upper lip, obviously designed to give the appearance of age and maturity but which in fact simply exaggerated his vulnerability. As they were engrossed in the task of splitting the food and pouring the steaming coffee, Langan shook his head. Boys like these were now the backbone of the US military. The hardened battle veterans from both sides of the Civil War, the bloodiest bitter conflict that had ever shaken that continent, had almost to a man been killed in the Indian wars, died or retired.

'Enjoy the food, soldiers,' exhorted Langan, deliberately avoiding the term 'boys'.'

'We will, sir,' said Silverstone. 'This is mighty good of you.'

'Think nothing of it. I'll be going into town soon. I guess you'll be coming with me.'

'Yes sir, we will. We got orders from the major himself not to let you out of our sight for a minute just in case you really do know these Indians.'

'And then we got to hightail it back as fast as we can to let the major know,' Lyon added.

'And a mighty fine job you are making of it. I'll make sure the major hears about it.'

Both appeared pleased with this commendation but then Lyon raised a concern.

'Mr Langan, is that black fellow going to be going with you? I mean, we were told to watch the two of you. So that's going to be pretty hard if you split up.'

'No, Mr Clay isn't coming with me. He's had a pretty hard time so he needs to rest up. But I give you my word that he's not going to be sloping off to meet any Indians.'

The fear of losing the support of the other soldier persuaded them to accept Langan's word and when the buggy passed them an hour or so later they both fell in behind it.

Billy Bob Hickey was still nursing his wrath about his half-brother when Little Bob's jaw thumped into his chest and his mouth remained wide open. He had stopped sweeping the boardwalk outside the jailhouse. As soon as he confirmed that his eyes were not deceiving him, he screamed:

'Sheriff, Sheriff. It's Langan.'

The sheriff, propelled by his hate, immediately jumped out of his seat and came to the door. He watched the buggy draw up.

'Well, look what the wind has blown

into town.' he proclaimed and then his eyes were pulled to Rebecca. He doffed his hat and said to her. 'Afternoon, Mrs. Langan. You're getting over your loss, I hope.' He laughed to himself before turning to the driver. 'Langan, did I not make myself clear enough when I told you how bad it would be for you if you stayed around?'

'Oh you did, indeed, Sheriff. Very clear indeed. Particularly with that little abduction yesterday. But as you can see I'm still perfectly healthy and I know now for sure who killed my father. That scurrilous good-for-nothing that you sent to do your dirty work has escaped justice. I'm going to make sure that you don't.'

A small crowd of townspeople had started to gather on the other side of the street, gazes fixed at the simmering altercation and wondering why the lawyer seemed to be shouting at the sheriff. Hickey looked across at them and even though he adjudged them to be out of earshot, he stepped closer to the buggy before speaking.

'Abduction? Tried to kill you? Mister, those are mighty serious allegations. And after I sent poor old Pete to look after you and he ends up dead.'

Langan was initially puzzled as to how the sheriff could have obtained this information so quickly. He remained silent. Hickey continued in a low whispering voice.

'I know what happened to Peter. I've lost a good man. What I don't know is what part you played in his murder. You brave enough to come into the jailhouse again and we can talk man to man?'

'Let's go.'

The enthusiasm with which Langan agreed surprised the sheriff. He had heard about these people who had a death wish, who had given up all concern for their own safety. Soldiers who would be the first to rise from their shelter and charge into battle directly in front of the enemy's cannons; condemned prisoners who had to be held back from running to the scaffold. He had never met one before. At least not until now, that was. He stepped back to allow Langan to jump down; he in turn walked around to help Rebecca disembark. As they were following Hickey through the door Langan suddenly halted and as the sheriff turned around, he advised:

'Only fair to tell you, Sheriff, I ain't Daniel walking into the lion's den. I have an escort now. Troopers Lyon and Silverstone. See them? So if anything happens to us you're going to have to answer to the cavalry.' He pointed to the two uniformed horsemen some way down the street.

Hickey looked at them through screwed up eyes.

'I want to find out exactly what you did to Peter before I kill you,' he hissed.

When they were inside the jailhouse, John went straight to the door that led to the cells. The two prisoners arrested during the fracas on the previous night threw an expectant look at him. They were now sober and hungry, but he pulled the door shut on them without returning their gaze.

Now isolated from any other witnesses, Langan was invited to relate his account of his escape. He did this briefly but chose to leave out all references to Edmund. When he had finished Hickey threw a cold hard stare at him.

'So you wanted a chance to gloat before you left town, did you?'

Langan shook his head. 'Sheriff, you have got it so mightily wrong. This is not about gloating. I am not going anywhere now until I ensure that the authorities know the truth about what happened up in Blackies Canyon.'

'Is that right now? Well you are an even bigger fool than I took you for. So what you figuring on doing next then, Mr Fancy Lawyer.'

'You will find out soon enough, anyway. I'm going to travel down to the courthouse at Boise and sign an affidavit in front of the county judge. Then I guess you might be getting a visit from one of the Territory marshals. I'm hoping, Hickey, that the next time I see your sorry face is when I look at you across a court room.'

The incongruous laugh from Hickey was the indicator that he had chosen this moment to retrieve the card that he had been keeping up his sleeve.

'They ain't going to believe you. It'll be your word against mine and I still have two deputies who plainly heard me advising a greenhorn not to go up country by himself.' A moment of uneasy silence hung in the air. 'But I'm glad you came to see me first,' he continued, 'because there is something that I guess you don't know, Langan. Let's just say that by some strange twist of fate they did believe you . . . ' The laugh had subsided but only as far as a broad smile and he let this play silently on his lips for a few moments before the trump card was banged down onto the table of their discussion ' . . . it would mean that Mrs. Langan would also find herself on a scaffold.'

Rebecca gasped in surprise at the mention of her name.

'What do you mean?' she blurted out. 'What are you talking about?'

'Come on now, Mrs Langan,' continued Hickey. 'We can be honest. You remember that when I told you about old man Langan's intention to change his will and leave you destitute, you came up with that idea of bushwhacking him before he could do anything of the kind. You told me how it was you that built up Far Fields and how it was so unfair that this upstart here would take it all away from you.'

'That's not true, that's not true,' protested Rebecca vehemently.

The sheriff's laugh returned. He had won this terrible game of poker.

'How else would you have known about the will? I got Milo as a witness to overhearing Pat talking about it. Then, he told my deputy, who, of course, told me. And when I came out to see you I was shown in by Maria. She would have heard me asking if you was real sure that you wanted me to make it right and she would have heard you say 'yes'. All of that is able to be proved in a court of law. She ain't going to lie on the Holy Bible is she, a good religious girl like her? Up till then I had no motive to kill your husband. Sure I was sweet on you, the whole town knew that, but by then you and Langan had split up so that wouldn't have made me kill him. It was because you asked me to kill him. That's the only reason. Maybe I was so besotted by you that I was driven to do it out of madness.'

Smirking broadly he turned to Langan. 'What's your professional advice? Do you think that if I pleaded insanity I might get off with it and leave just Mrs Langan with the hangman?'

As Rebecca listened to this she had felt a heavy weight grow in her mouth and place itself precariously over her throat. It now plunged deep into her stomach and she grimaced. When she looked up again she could only see the inane grin on Hickey's face staring mockingly at her. She stepped forward, her hand raised to slap him but he blocked the blow with his own arm and pushed her backwards. As Langan positioned himself in between them, Billy Bob also moved towards him.

But the sheriff appeared to be completely untroubled by the attempted assault and continued speaking in a slow measured voice.

'You have any idea at all, Mrs Langan, what it's like to meet the hangman? First of all that old rope just rubs and rubs against your neck. Loose strands kind of tickle and you are just begging to be able to scratch, but of course you can't because your hands are tied up behind your back. Then the noose is pulled tight, so tight your tongue pops out and you are fighting for your last breath of air. Then you hear a loud crack at the back of your neck and — '

'Stop it!' screamed Langan.

He put his arm around Rebecca who had now started to sob and pulled her closer to him. As Hickey observed this, his hatred was nourished.

'Well, I've finished anyway. 'Cos nobody has ever come back from the grave to tell us what the next bit is like.'

'You'll find out for yourself, soon enough, Sheriff,' rasped Langan.

'Don't think so, Mr Langan. But I'm getting bored by this conversation. So Billy Bob there will show you to the buggy and we'll make sure that all the folks outside see how healthy you are. And if you want to stay that way, I'd advise you to get the next train out of here.'

Billy Bob was holding the door open now and the two figures walked through it. Langan removed his arm from Rebecca's shoulder and turned around.

'That's not an option.'

'Well then, the only other option you have is to call me out and I'll be looking forward to that.'

As soon as they were both inside the buggy, Langan removed the whip and gave the horses an uncharacteristic lash to their rumps. The dust from the speeding wagon filled the air and Hickey watched it travel out of town until it disappeared from view.

They travelled in silence but inside Langan's head different voices shouted and screamed. In a vain effort to dismiss them, he drove the horses harder and harder. Rebecca clung tightly to the black iron side-rail and the two escorting cavalrymen had to gallop hard to keep them in sight. It was only when they reached the bridge that marked the start of Far Fields that Langan slowed down. After a few minutes of awkward silence he spoke.

'What did Hickey mean when he said calling him out was the only other option?'

'Challenging him to a gun fight,' she explained. 'But that would be madness.'

'This is all madness,' he replied.

Then the question that had been simmering inside his mind, the one that had risen above all of the other voices, was spoken at last.

'That story of Hickey's, the one about you being behind Pat's murder, it's not true, is it?'

She deliberately moved around in her seat to look into his face before she answered. 'No, of course it isn't. How could you even entertain the slightest doubt?'

'It's what he said about motive that sounded pretty convincing. Pat said that he hadn't spoken to anyone about changing the will so I wondered how you knew.'

'Alright, you need to know what happened. Hickey did come and see me to tell me that. And at the time I was pretty upset. You know how important Far Fields is to me, but it certainly was never so important that I would have had any part in killing Pat. Hickey did ask me if I wanted him to sort everything out and I might have given him the impression that I did. But he never mentioned murder. I had no idea that that was what he was talking about. At worst, I guessed that he was talking about encouraging you to leave town. I didn't even think about that conversation after I heard about Pat's death. You have to believe me.' She now had a firm grip on his sleeve as she repeated: 'You have to believe me.'

'I do, Rebecca, but I am not convinced that a county judge would. There's just enough of Hickey's version that can be substantiated to create some doubt.'

'But that means Hickey will have won. He will have got away with murder.'

'Hell, I was only bluffing. I wasn't at all sure that I was going to go down to Boise. I've already had one experience of trying to convince somebody about my story and it just didn't wash with Major Kaisen. Just because I write it down it doesn't mean that folks are going to take it any more seriously. There's no substantive evidence. As the sheriff says, it's his word against mine and I'm the stranger around these parts.'

She stared at him as he rubbed her cheek with the palm of his hand.

'But now the stakes are raised,' he continued. 'It's not just a case of nobody believing me or even running me out of town for making malicious allegations against the sheriff. Hickey is correct, there is a real risk that if he was convicted, they would believe his implication of you. Confessions of condemned men seem to be given a pretty high credibility. Maybe they think that once people have nothing else to lose, they just try to make their peace with God. But low-life scum like Hickey would take his grudge to the grave. I'm sure of that. So it's too big a risk. Far too big a risk.'

She smiled an awkward little smile. 'OK. I know you had to make your own mind up but I can't say that I'm not glad. That means that you and I can leave this place. Put all of that horror behind us. The ranch will just about run itself and allow you to show me these fine cities, back East.'

'Rebecca, I can't walk away like that. It's hard enough already for me to lay my head down on the pillow every night. It would be a hundred times worse if I didn't do the right thing this time.'

Her voice was raised as she asked: 'So what are you going to do?'

'Precisely what the sheriff suggested. Challenge him to a gun fight.'

She wondered whether she should laugh at his joke but saw in his face that he was completely serious.

'No,' she gasped, 'you can't. You don't even carry a gun.'

'Just because I don't carry one doesn't mean I can't shoot them, you know. I learned how to fire a pistol back in New York.'

'So you ever shot a man before?'

'No, of course not.'

'There's a world of difference looking along your sights into another man's eyes and firing at some straw target.'

'Don't think I haven't thought this through. I stopped seeing Hickey as a man, sometime during that period I was trussed up over a horse being carried up to my intended murder. And besides, I have got an important friend on my side — surprise. Hickey won't be expecting me to ride into town tomorrow to challenge him and with a bit of luck, he might go over to the Silver Dollar tonight to celebrate sending me away with my tail between my legs.'

He was now pulling on the reins to bring the buggy to a halt in front of the ranch house. She spoke quietly to seek confirmation.

'Tomorrow morning? You are going to call him out tomorrow morning?'

'Yes. If I leave it any later, I might get cold feet.'

'But what if . . . ' she hesitated before concluding the sentence, ' . . . he kills you?'

'Then I'll die one death, but if I run away I'll die a thousand deaths.'

16

Rebecca had run sobbing into the house as Langan took off the harness and led the pair to the stable. He caught sight of Edmund at the far end of the yard and waved him over.

'Edmund, take care of these horses and then see if you can find Pat's pistols.'

When Edmund returned he saw the five bottles sitting on top of the fence posts that marked the perimeter of the yard.

'These what you are looking for?'

Langan affirmed with a nod but before the set of Colt 45s and their holsters were passed over, Edmund enquired:

'You ever fired one of these before, Mr Langan?'

Langan did not get an opportunity to respond as the foreman continued:

'Before you shoot, you gotta palm the hammer back like this.' The short curled piece of metal at the top of the handle was pulled backwards in the flat of Edmund's hand. It gave a reassuring click when it reached its station and the barrel containing the bullet chambers rotated one space around. 'See, it's loaded again now, ready to fire. Some folk are able to pull it back with their thumb and so they can fire both pistols at the same time, but I reckon you would be better just using one of the guns like I showed you.'

'Thanks for the advice. But I'm not completely unfamiliar with thumb-breakers,' Langan said as he strapped on the shiny leather belt. His hands gripped the gleaming mother-of-pearl handles to seize the revolvers from their holsters. The muzzles of each glistened as though they had been newly polished. He returned one of the single-action pistols to its pouch and focused his attention on the other, pulling back the hammer and releasing the catch to let the wheel fall free. He spun it around in the palm of his hand and when it came to rest, inserted a shell in each of the six chambers. He then walked back a few steps.

'What do you reckon, Edmund?' he shouted. 'This about the distance between the hotel and the jailhouse?'

'About it, Mr Langan,' opined his companion.

The extended arm pointed towards the first bottle as he squeezed the trigger. The bullet shot over the receptacle by about six inches.

'Bit more recoil than I expected,' Langan commented.

He fired again and this time the bottle was smashed into pieces. He quickly disposed of the other four by the same means.

'Waow! You were right, you have shot before. I sure am glad about that.'

'You know what all this is about, then?'

'I had to ask Mrs Langan for the guns. They were stacked away in a drawer in the boss's bedroom,' explained Edmund. 'She asked me not to get them for you and told me what you're going to do. She's a good woman, you know. She's real worried about you. That notion about her cheating on the boss, it was all in his head.'

Langan's teeth slid hard into his bottom lip to prevent himself making any comment.

'I told her that you would get a set of guns anyway,' Edmund continued, 'and that you may as well have good ones. Boss took care of these beauties. Always greasing them and keeping the sights right. So she ended up givin' them to me but told me that you had gone crazy.'

'And you think I'm mad too, do you?'

Edmund shrugged his shoulders in a gesture of resignation.

'I guess you have to do what you feel is right, but the sheriff is a mighty mean critter. Even though you can shoot, he's going to try and get the draw on you.'

'And he might just do that, which is why I'm hoping that we'll be fifty or so yards apart. Even though he might get his gun out first. I'm banking on having a better aim.'

'I'll say one thing for you, Mr Langan. You got your father's guts.'

Jack Langan smiled and placed his hand on Edmund's shoulder.

'You know there was another Edmund who used to say a lot of clever things. A man called Edmund Burke; he's been dead a long time now, but I read some of his writings at law school. And some of his words just keep on going around and around in my head.'

'What words are those, Mr Langan?'

The lawyer looked out to the distance and quoted: '*The only thing necessary for the triumph of evil is for good men to do nothing.*'

Rebecca hardly spoke a word that evening and retired shortly after dinner. Langan fell asleep in a chair and woke well before dawn. Even so, Rebecca was already in the kitchen when he entered, dressed and obviously expecting to accompany him. As soon as she saw him she spoke.

'I've sent Maisie up to the soldiers with some hot food and to check that they are not still sleeping when you set out. I guessed you would want to make sure that they were with you when you go into town.'

He tried to laugh. 'Sure do! Don't want any of those deputies plugging me in the back before I get a chance to face their boss.'

He noticed how red and puffy her eyes were as he declined the offer of breakfast.

'I don't want any food. Just fix me some strong coffee. I need to get this thing over and done with, so we can all stop suffering.'

She went to put a cup on the table but it fell and smashed on the stone floor. This served to precipitate the flood of tears that she had been bottling up. He hugged her tightly and tried to reassure her.

'Don't worry. I know what I am doing. Don't cry for me. I have been given a chance to get back my self-respect.' He looked at the riding-breeches that she was wearing and continued: 'But you have to under-stand, this is something I have to do by myself. I need you to wait here. I would only be worried about you if you came and I need to have my mind set completely on the gunfight. Believe me, I'll be back.'

Just as the sun rose over the horizon and brought its warming, life-giving rays down on Far Fields, Langan set off in the buggy, with his now ever-present cavalry escort to face his potential death square on. When he reached the town, it was still early in the morning but the double gates of the livery stable were in the process of being flung wide open. Langan caught sight of the blacksmith and requested that someone rub his horses down and give them some hay and water. The blacksmith's jaw dropped wide open as he watched Langan reach into the back of the buggy to retrieve a set of holsters and belt the two pistols tightly to his waist.

17

Langan was correct. Hickey had gone out to celebrate the previous night and had only just reached the jailhouse that morning when the sound of a pistol crack shattered the air. Stripped to the waist, he was standing over a metal basin washing his body. He stood up quickly and pulling his braces over his bare shoulders, stepped towards the door. He stood staring at Langan. The pistol was still being held aloft, barrel pointing towards the sky and smoke drifting from its mouth.

Hickey rubbed his bleary eyes and let loose a burst of mocking laughter.

'Langan, you've gone and got yourself a pair of shooting irons,' he shouted. 'You want to be careful, they can be mighty dangerous in the wrong hands.'

'I'm wearing these, Hickey, because

you are a murdering liar.'

'Words are easy, Langan. You man enough to back them up?'

'I'm calling you out, Sheriff. Are you man enough to take that challenge?'

A small crowd had converged outside the barber's shop on the other side of the street. It was growing quickly, straining to hear what was happening.

'That's Pat Langan's son,' someone explained to anyone who hadn't recognized Jack.

'He wants to challenge the sheriff to a gun fight,' gasped another member of this assembly. A mother tried to pull her son into the folds of her dress and cover his eyes but the boy resisted and remained transfixed on the scene in front of him.

'But he's from back East. He doesn't carry a gun,' added Milo, the hotel clerk, who had been on his way to the Metropole when the curtain rose on this theatre.

'What's going on between him and the sheriff?' enquired the mother.

'He just called the sheriff a murdering liar,' related Milo.

Someone at the back of the crowd muttered that he might be correct and a number of heads nodded in silent agreement.

The sheriff raised his eyes above Langan and addressed the group of observers.

'You all hear that? Mr.Langan has made some bad allegations about me and wants to back them up with a gunfight. Well, if a fair fight is what he wants, then a fair fight is what he is going to get. You are all witnesses to Langan's call.'

Then he addressed the other gladiator. 'Give me five minutes to finish my ablutions and get dressed. It'll give you time to make your peace with your maker. I'll be right with you and we can sort out this business between us once and for all.'

The sheriff went back into the jailhouse before Langan turned. As the lawyer walked slowly up the middle of the street, he could feel the eyes of the deputies and the crowd burn into his back. When he was level with the hotel, he stopped. The two young cavalrymen were now just ahead of him, bemused with all of that morning's events. They had no idea why Langan had challenged the sheriff but returned his nod and then made sure that they were protected from any stray bullets or ricochets.

Langan turned again facing the direction from which he had just come. The sun was behind him and if anything it would be a hindrance to Hickey. He had tried to stack the cards in his favour as much as he legitimately could. Moments later, the sheriff marched out of the jailhouse and into that dusty arena. He was now fully dressed and wearing a black leather waistcoat that was ostentatiously embellished by the silver star of his badge of office.

The men stood square on to each other. The sheriff's wide-brimmed hat cast a shadow over his features but as Langan looked deep into the face of his adversary even from that distance, he recognized the stare of hate and spite. But he also saw the face of a man who had lived a life that he was going to attempt to extinguish. He knew that he would be trying to make Hickey's wife a widow. He wondered whether she would grieve. He wondered too whether there were any children whom he would be turning into orphans. Who would grieve for this man, who would cry at his funeral and who would remember him long after his body had turned to dust?

His thoughts were rudely disturbed by Langan's shout.

'You ready now, Langan?'

Langan pulled his pistol out of its holster as quickly as he could but he still felt Hickey's first bullet whiz past his left ear. He had spun his body through ninety degrees and now had the gun levelled. He was staring down the sight trying to hold the weapon steady. Hickey was moving towards him. Although Langan had only shot at targets at the gun club, he had listened to the more experienced members talking about using weapons to kill men. These were the military officers, Union and Confederate, who had fought at Gettysburg, Shiloh and Fredericksburg. Turn side on, they had advised, that way you reduce your opponent's target area. Aim for the single biggest visible area, the chest, they had exhorted. Don't bother about trying to pinpoint the heart or anything else. A bullet anywhere in the upper body would generally render a man *hors de combat* even if it didn't kill him outright.

As he was about to squeeze the trigger he felt what seemed like a punch to his right shoulder. His hand involuntarily jerked into the air and the gun was propelled out of his grasp. He watched it describe a gravity-defying semicircle before falling to the earth. And then saw the blood start to spurt out of the wound. Although he felt no pain, only a warm sensation spreading down his arm, he instinctively pushed his left hand over the open hole in his shoulder. Still the blood seeped through his fingers. He cursed himself. A true gunfighter would have been sufficiently ambidextrous to reach automatically for his left-hand pistol to continue the battle.

Now, it was too late. Hickey had covered about half of the distance that had separated them at the beginning of the duel. He discharged his gun for a third time. The bullet crashed into his kneecap and Langan heard the sound of bone splintering as he fell to the ground. At least it didn't seem to be bleeding in the same way; the pain prevented him from pulling himself to his feet again. He buried his face in the ground, spitting out the dust that had been blown into his mouth. As he lay there, the world seemed to attain a glorious stillness. He braced himself in expectation of the final piece of hot pointed metal that would dispatch him to that true Supreme Court. Death would only be a passing moment, he told himself. He hoped that his life would be judged fairly, that the good that he had done and the stances he had taken would be set against the disappointments and failures. Perhaps the soul of his wife would be called as witness, but he was unsure whether it would be for the defence or the prosecution.

'Well Mr High and Mighty, that's sure knocked you off your perch, hasn't it?' Hickey's shadow towered above him and he watched the wisp of smoke drift lazily out of the muzzle. The smell of gunpowder assailed his nostrils and suddenly he felt a kick being delivered to his ribs. He let out a low groan as the toe-piece dug under the bones and then saw his gun resting uselessly a few feet from him. Hickey caught him looking at it and for a moment the two men held each other in a stare. On this stage and in that split second in time each man saw the other as the most important thing in his life. The prospective killer and his potential victim.

Then Hickey's eyes flicked and with the side of his boot he kicked the hope of salvation even further away from the man who had challenged him. Then he set his eyes on Langan again.

'You ain't dead yet,' he said. 'Sure, a couple of scratches. That's all for now. But you are going to die and as you do, I want you to think about Peter.'

'That piece of scum got all that he deserved,' hissed Langan through gritted teeth. He received another kick in acknowledgement that he had been heard.

'Listen up good, Langan, till I tell you how it's going to be. I'm going to kill you, that's for sure. But I'm figurin' on doing it slowly. I'm going to put another couple of bullets into that useless body of yours and let you bleed to death like a hog.'

The crowd had now moved up the street and from the safety of the boardwalk and about twenty yards distance was straining to hear the discussion between these two combatants. Hickey noticed that Doc Morrison was at the vanguard of the seething mass of townspeople with his trademark black bag. He should have already learned, thought Hickey, that his ministrations would be rendered superfluous. A coffin would be all that was ever going to be required.

The sheriff, with his pistol still pointing, bent down to speak in a lower voice, a voice that wouldn't be overheard by the rabble behind him.

'But you got another way out, Langan. You can reach for your other gun and when I shoot you again, I'll make sure that the end is quick and clean. You never know, you might just get lucky. And to tell you the whole truth, it's better for me too. Crowd over there might get a little spooked at the sight of me killing a disarmed man.'

The figure on the ground painfully

turned around to look into his tormentor's eyes.

'Rot in hell, Hickey,' he spat.

The sheriff jumped up with a surprising alacrity and pumped another bullet into Langan's right shin. From that point-blank range, it passed straight through the limb and lodged itself in the ground. As the sheriff stood back to admire his sadistic torture, both men heard the clatter of hoofs pounding down the street. They turned to see Rebecca pull tightly on the reins of her palomino and dismount with a single leap. She sprinted between the two adversaries shouting at Hickey.

'Stop it. Stop it. Leave him alone. You've won. We'll both quit town, the Territory, for ever, and let you get on with what you do here.'

Then she bent over Langan, her eyes welling up with tears.

'I couldn't wait back at the ranch,' she said. 'I was so worried what might happen to you. Don't be angry with me.'

'I'm not angry with you. You are far too important for me to be angry,' Langan said in a weak croaky voice.

Hickey was towering over them as he listened. If only she had had a portion of the feelings she harboured for Langan reserved for him, he contemplated, then this whole story would have turned out so differently. Jealousy as well as hate consumed him. He interrupted their tryst to answer her offer of self-imposed exile.

'Can't do it. Can't deal any more. It's too late for that. It was Langan's call. Now I've got to kill him. I can't let the town see their sheriff challenged like that without sorting it out. Folks would think that their sheriff had gone soft and someone else might try calling me out, too.'

She was struggling to help the bleeding body to its feet and the sheriff suddenly realized that she was blocking the view of Hickey's other gun. He became agitated and a sweat broke out on his brow.

'Stand away. Stand away, Rebecca. This business ain't finished yet. You hear me now,' he ordered, and then pointed his pistol at her head.

She turned around to face him.

'You will have to shoot me first, Sheriff,' she said.

The sheriff's lips curled at one end and he spat.

'If that's what it takes, then that's what'll be. Langan knew what he was doing. It was never a pissing competition.' He pointed his pistol straight at Rebecca's head but she continued to hold him in an ice-cold stare.

'Rebecca, get out of the way. He's serious,' screamed Langan painfully. 'He hasn't got anything more to lose.'

'Neither have I,' she responded curtly.

The crowd gasped when they heard the click of the hammer load another bullet but then an unexpected shout tore through the air.

'That's enough, Hickey. There'll be no more shooting today,' Morrison screamed as he stepped forward and stood beside Rebecca.

'Get the hell out of here,' commanded the lawman. 'It's no business of yours.' But the doctor didn't move.

'You going to shoot me as well, are you? How many bodies do you need to see lying out here on the street before you are satisfied? The whole town's just about had enough of you, Hickey.'

Collective murmurings from the crowd confirmed his last statement and the doctor opened the black bag to begin work on Langan's wounds. Hickey continued to watch the small gathering in numb disbelief at what was occurring. As he stood there someone in the crowd hurled a rock at him. It hit him on the shoulder and bounced on to the ground. Morrison stopped momentarily to look at the missile and then returned to the task of applying bandages.

'Who threw that?' shrieked the sheriff as he faced the group of townspeople. He could not help but notice that its numbers seemed to have become vastly swollen over the preceding few minutes. No one admitted the offence but of even greater concern for the sheriff was the fact that the crowd had no inclination to identify the perpetrator. It appeared as though it had united in a defiant gesture.

'Closing ranks,' sneered Hickey. 'Well that ain't going to get you very far, 'cos I'll find out who is responsible and when I do they are going to feel mighty sore.'

John and Little Bob had now come off the boardwalk and joined their boss. Both had rifles primed and held across their chests.

'This don't look too good,' commented John.

'Keep your mouth shut and your gun ready, John.' Hickey's eyes scoured the sea of faces until they rested upon familiar features. 'Jess Patton, I see you there. You are going to tell me who threw that rock.'

'I didn't see anything, Sheriff.'

'Don't believe you, Jess! You tell me what I want to know or I'll arrest you.'

The tone of the response was characterised by defiance rather than the fear that Hickey had anticipated.

'I told you that I don't know, but even if I did, I wouldn't be telling you. Your bullying has gone on for far too long.'

Hickey turned around to John but in tones designed for a wider audience, he exclaimed:

'You hear that? You hear the way he speaks to me? Go and pull him out and take him down the jailhouse so that we can teach him some manners.'

As the two deputies started to move, the crowd surged forward. A sea of faces hissed and spat at them and then another rock was hurled from the back. It caught Billy Bob on the chest and forced him back on to his heels. John let his rifle fall to his side and his finger curled a little bit more around the trigger. Still the mob came forward and steadily they inched towards the lawmen, moving in from the right and left.

'Shoot them, shoot into the crowd,' called his brother.

The deputy turned around, his eyes open as wide as they would go and his jaw hanging down in a dual statement of disbelief and fear.

'They're our neighbours. There's women and children in there. We can't shoot.'

'Don't you argue none with me. Do as I say,' barked the sheriff.

'Billy Bob, if we kill anyone, they'll hunt us down like animals. The army won't be looking for any redskins any more, they'll be after us.'

Hickey realized immediately the sense of his brother's argument. He took his other gun out its holster and fired two shots into the air. This caused the crowd to freeze and about forty pairs of eyes turned to Hickey to see what he would do next. They were all surprised when he wrenched off the silver star and threw it onto the ground.

'If that's how people feel, you can go and get yourself a new sheriff,' he shouted. 'I won't stand in your way but just don't come crying to me when the miners bust up the town or when some rustlers run away with your cattle.'

The three lawmen backed out of the only part of the circle that hadn't been closed by the surrounding throng and headed for the jailhouse.

'What are we going to do now?' came the plaintive childlike plea from Little Bob as soon as they reached the protection of their bastion and had slammed the door firmly shut. Both deputies looked to the former sheriff for an answer.

'We'll hightail it into the hills for a few days. We need horses and provisions.'

'Sure, Billy Bob. I'll go and fetch them.'

Little Bob would have passed through the door had Hickey not grabbed him.

'What you call me there, Deputy? You

199

are being mighty familiar, ain't you? You address me as 'Sheriff' all the time. You hear me now?'

Before responding, Little Bob cast a furtive glance at his half-brother, who shrugged his shoulders in a manner that indicated that he shared the confusion.

'But you just gave them your badge back. You ain't the sheriff any more . . . are you?'

'Returning the badge meant nothing. Once there is a little bit of trouble here, the townsfolk are going to be begging for us to put on our badges again.'

When it was time to quit town, however, they left by the back door of the jailhouse.

18

The doctor called some of the men out of the crowd to carry the invalid to his surgery. Rebecca followed on behind. As the bearers laid Langan out on the couch, he grimaced and let out a yelp before cursing. The doctor shouted for hot water and then addressed his patient.

'Don't be angry with the pain. The fact that you feel sore is good. It tells you that you are alive. And after calling Hickey out, well, that's quite a bonus. You sure are a lucky man. The bullet to the knee means you'll need a stick for a while but the other two are just flesh wounds. Once I patch you up, you'll go straight back to the ranch and rest up.'

'How long am I going to have to stay there?' the patient enquired.

'Depends on how fast you heal and how much blood you lost. I'll look in in a couple of days and with a bit of luck you could be up and moving by the end of the week. Ain't nothing that's so important that can't wait that long, is there?'

'I guess that there isn't,' answered Langan.

The Hickey boys stayed in the saddle for the remainder of that day, compelled more by the frustration of defeat rather than an urge to arrive somewhere. They stopped off at one of the small farms to steal some chickens and when dusk began to descend they found a spot to set up camp on the side of the mountain. They were less than six miles from their starting-point back in Franklin.

They gathered up some wood and built a fire on which they would cook. Billy Bob retrieved a couple of bottles of whiskey from his saddlebag and sat down to wash the sour taste of that day's events out of his mouth.

The flames served as a beacon all across the valley. On the other side of that gigantic bowl, five Indians huddled in a cave watched the night sky light up.

In front of the camp-fire Billy Bob was becoming more maudlin. He prodded the flames with a long stick and raked the ashes without any purpose being served, as he delivered his thoughts.

'It ain't fair, after all we have done for that town. I've given them my life. And Langan's widow ain't never ought to have taken to that fancy lawyer,' he asserted. 'She needs a real man, someone who knows the ways of these parts.'

'Like you, Billy Bob,' commented his sycophantic half-brother.

'Yeah! Just like me. But instead she had to fall for that sweet-talking lawyer from back East. You know that we are going to have to kill him, don't you, boys? He ain't no longer just some plumb loco greenhorn. He's the man who challenged the sheriff.'

'So how you figuring on doing that now?' asked Little Bob.

Hickey's stare was held on the licking flames of the fire as though they were joined by an invisible steel rod. Suddenly he exploded.

'Fire. We'll burn the whole place down to the ground. I reckon they will take him back to Far Fields to let him recuperate a bit. So we got to act quickly, tomorrow, no later than tomorrow.'

John and Little Bob were looking at the sheriff but his eyes reached past them and into the darkness. His voice sounded as though he was speaking to some distant listener as he continued: 'If we go after the cowboys have set about their business for the day, there'll only be the women there.'

'But won't folk know that it was us who did,' worried John.

'Not if they see some Indians around again. We all know that they are prowling around Langan's lands. The hungrier they get, the bolder they'll get. Just a matter of time before the real Indians burn down the ranch house, particularly when they find out that for most of the day there's only some women and a sick old man there.' He turned to Little Bob. 'You could find those buckskins again. Couldn't you?'

A broad smile accompanied the response.

'Sure could, Sheriff. We dressing up again?'

John's interjection was less enthusiastic.

'You forgot about the escort. Those two cavalrymen who are following Langan around.'

The sheriff rubbed his chin in contemplation when he grunted, 'So much the better, because they can then witness that it was the Indians.'

'Don't you think that they might try to protect Langan?'

'No.' Billy Bob smirked. 'No, I don't. Patton told me that he was speaking to them. They are just frightened boys. They'll hightail it as soon as they catch sight of any Indians. That's their orders. Major Kaisen is only interested in catching and hanging the Indians. He don't give a cuss about protecting Langan.'

The implications of the sheriff's plan registered in John's mind and his face creased with anxiety.

'We are going to let the women escape though, ain't we?'

Billy Bob's look was one of disparagement.

'We can't. The Indians wouldn't let them escape and besides there's a chance they might recognize us. Don't want us getting rid of one person who can put a noose around our necks and leaving three others. No, they got to go as well.'

John stood up and took a deep breath before he spoke.

'I'm your brother and I've got to say this. I can't keep quiet any longer. Sorting out cowboys or miners who break the law is one thing but we can't go around killing innocent folks, particularly when they're women. I think we should just call it quits and get out of here.'

Billy Bob did not believe what he was hearing. He also raised himself and walked over to his brother. He continued his approach until his face was right up at John's nose.

'I'm getting mighty worried about you, brother. Back there in Franklin you disobeyed my orders when I told you to shoot into the crowd. And now you think it's quits with Langan after what he did to Peter? You think it's quits when he made us leave town like that. It ain't quits till I know that he's dead. You hear me now?'

John resisted blinking and continued to hold his stare.

'Then this is where we split up, Billy Bob. I'm not coming with you.'

He had barely finished speaking when his brother's rage exploded and he felt the fist crash into his jaw. He was rocked backwards.

'You yellow-bellied coward. You ain't no brother of mine,' the sheriff screamed as he grabbed John and punched him again. Had it not been for the large boulder directly behind him, John would have fallen to the ground. He could feel blood in his mouth but managed to propel himself forward, running right into his brother. Billy Bob gave out a low groan and lifted his knee in two sharp jerks into his assailant's chest. John winced. He was still holding on and wrestled the sheriff to the ground. Then the brothers rolled around the earth as though they were two halves of the same ball. But the strength of the younger man started to pay off as Billy Bob became tired and gasped for breath. John gained the upper position and sat on top of his brother. He pinned his arms to the ground with his knees.

His hands were now around the sheriff's neck and both of his thumbs pressed as hard as he could against the windpipe. Billy Bob's face turned blue and he could only splutter a mixture of incomprehensible words and spit in between the frantic gasps for air. The idea of pressing even harder until he had forced all of the life out of his brother consumed John's thoughts. But he could not dismiss from his mind the knowledge that it was his own flesh and blood he was choking. His grip relaxed. He let himself fall off and unsteadily pulled himself to his feet. Billy Bob was still coughing and wheezing as John walked over and started to roll up his blanket.

'That looks like that's the finish between us. I'll be on my way.'

He was leaning over his bag and had his back to the fire. He never saw Billy Bob creep up on him, holding his gun like a hammer. And then with all the strength that the vanquished could muster, the sheriff brought the handle of his pistol down on his brother's head. John crumbled to the ground. Billy Bob had to kneel down to continue pistol-whipping him.

Little Bob had watched all of the fight, confused and worried. He moved over and awkwardly stood between Billy

Bob and his victim. Billy Bob tried to push him out of the way, but he grabbed the hand holding the weapon.

'Sheriff, you are going to kill him,' he cried. 'You are going to kill John.'

When he realized that his hand was trapped in a grip that was too strong for him to release, the sheriff raised himself to his full height.

'You do it then,' he barked. 'Get the gun and you kill him.'

'Sheriff, I can't do that to John. He's my kith and kin. You and him sure, you are all that I got in this world, now that Peter's gone.'

Billy Bob pointed his gun at the still figure on the ground.

'Get out the way then, you whimpering idiot. I'll do it myself.' He slowly began to squeeze the trigger but just before it reached the bite point after which there would be no return, no chance to retain that deadly missile in the safety of the chamber, his shaking body whipped around and the bullet flew harmlessly into the ground. His free hand reached up to his eyes and the rough skin swept away any trace of moisture but it continued to cover them for a few moments longer before he spoke.

'It seems like we are just going to have to leave him for the wolves or a grizzly. I can't shoot him either.'

Meanwhile the advancing Indians stopped and listened. The sound of a single gunshot told them they were close to the camp-fire.

The sheriff and Little Bob took the three horses and began their trek down the mountainside. When Hayin and his braves arrived, all they saw was an inert body and the fresh imprint of hoofs leading away. Hayin leaned over the body and confirmed that John was still breathing before receiving a leather water-pouch. He poured the contents over the unconscious body. Gradually the deputy opened his eyes. He peered at the painted face that was staring down at him and then sat up abruptly. Hayin drew a knife and approached.

John gasped and wondered what would happen to him but the medicine man merely tapped twice the tin badge that the deputy was still wearing.

'You are with the sheriff?' he asked.

Fear and panic continued to hold John in their frozen grip. He said nothing so Hayin carried on: 'You had a friend. The one that tried to kill the long man. And so we had to kill him.'

He nodded towards another brave who opened his sack and pulled out the scalp. At first it was too dark for John to recognize what he was being shown, but as the brave moved closer, he saw the shrivelled piece of skin with the strands of curly brown hair attached to it. He would have shrieked out loud but Hayin's hand moved quickly to cover his mouth and stifle any further sound.

'What do you want from me?' asked the terrified lawman.

'I don't know yet. It was you who guided us here by the flames in the night sky.'

'I don't know nothing. I have nothing to tell you.'

Hayin touched his head and felt hairs matted with dry blood.

'This tells me that is not so but it will be the only evidence of our meeting.'

The sharp point of the dagger pressed further into John's neck and a trickle of blood started to run down the outside of his throat.

'OK. I'll tell you. The sheriff is going to try and kill Langan again. Tomorrow. This time he is going to burn down the ranch house,' he whimpered.

'And you are not going with him?'

'No. I have had a bellyful of killing. It's gone on too long.'

The pressure from the knife was released and the medicine man stepped away.

'Go then,' he said. 'Find another way to live.'

John started to slink into the night. As he reached the end of the clearing he turned again to face Hayin.

'Are you going to kill the sheriff?' he asked.

'No. We have learned to walk in the paleface's world and not disturb a single blade of grass. We shall not interfere. It is our way. What will happen to the sheriff, will happen. He must face his own kind of justice, the white man's justice.'

'In that case,' declared John, 'I should tell you that the sheriff and his deputy will be wearing Indian clothes. They are going to try and blame the killing on you, again.'

The Indian merely nodded to him and then signalled to his braves that they had work to do that night.

19

On the same morning as the gunfight twelve Indian scouts arrived at the army camp and were taken to the commanding officer. 'Rest up and we'll set out at first light tomorrow. Just make sure you all stay off the firewater,' the major shouted to their leader, Speeding Arrow.

The army patrol set off at dawn and as soon as it cleared the town, headed up the rough track towards Blackies Canyon. The scouts spread out and looked for the tell-tale signs. When they found a broken twig, they broke another one and by comparison could tell the age of the fracture. In the soft mud of the bank of the stream they checked to see whether any stones had been pressed into the ground by the force of man or a horse passing over them. It did not take long though before one of them shouted and waved. Speeding Arrow and Major Kaisen converged upon him simultaneously. He was holding three strands of horsehair that he had found snagged on the branch of gorse-bush. Speeding Arrow turned to the Major.

'They have been here. And recently.'

'How do you know it was the Indians? Some cowhands could have been up this way. It could have come off their horses couldn't it?'

'No,' Speeding Arrow replied. 'This is from an Indian's horse. Feel it. The hair is not brushed smooth, the way white men brush the hair of their horses.'

Now all of the scouts dismounted and searched on their hands and knees for another tell-tale sign. Soon they found some broken pine needles and then very soon after that prints from an unshod horse.

'They are travelling in this direction,' Speeding Arrow told the major and watched the smile of vindication emerge. Within a mile they came to a large area of fields used to graze cattle. As the whole troop stood on the edge of this plain they could clearly see a path traced across the grass that had been pressed down as horses had been ridden over it.

Speeding Arrow brought his horse up next to the major's.

'Something is wrong. You have been looking for these Shoshone for over a moon. But today they shout from the mountaintop which road they travel. The grass has been trodden down this morning. Maybe just two or three hours ago, otherwise the wind would have blown it all back up.'

'Good. Good. We're gaining on them,' crowed Kaisen to the soldiers around them. But when the scout did not turn his mount to resume the hunt, he barked: 'Come on, man. Let's get after them. We'll have their necks stretched before today is finished.'

Speeding Arrow voiced his concern.

'It is too easy. There are too many signs. It's as though they are telling us to come this way. They want us to follow them. We shall not go any further. This is not tracking. This is following Shoshone directions.' The taste of success in finding his quarry was like a fine wine in the major's mouth. He had no intention of spitting it out.

'You will do exactly as I say,' exclaimed Kaisen. 'I'm ordering you to continue.'

Nichol suddenly realized that the route indicated by the flattened grass would take them in the direction of Far Fields ranch house. As he looked into the distance he saw the first trace of smoke rise gracefully and straight into the sky on that windless morning.

'I don't think we need the trackers any more, Major,' he shouted. 'Look over there.'

Kaisen also caught sight of the smoke.

'Where's it coming from?' he enquired of Nichol.

'I think it's the ranch house.'

Kaisen looked at the trail over the fields as it snaked its way in the direction of the smoke.

'So their Indian friends have burnt them out.'

Speeding Arrow sneered at the major and then rode off in the direction from which they had come. The other three trackers jumped on to the bare backs of their horses and whooping and yelling galloped past the line of astounded cavalrymen.

Nichol bent his head and responded to his commanding officer's last assertion.

'With respect, sir, we don't even yet know that it is the renegades who have started the fire.'

Kaisen ignored this comment to watch the Indian trackers ride into the distance.

'You are right, we don't need them any more. We know where the Indians will be.'

★ ★ ★

Under the cloak of darkness, the sheriff and Little Bob had returned to the jailhouse. They parcelled up the buckskins and headbands and slipped out into the night again. Now they were tired but their mission had been accomplished. As soon as they cleared the environs of Franklin they could find somewhere to rest up until morning. Perhaps even get a little sleep. They would not be disturbed. Since old man Langan's murder, ordinary townsfolk tended not to venture too far from the safety of the town.

When they woke, they brewed up some coffee and set off for Far Fields. Just before the last clearing, they changed into the Indian clothes and then rounded the corner of the drive. The two young horsemen were still sitting under the oak tree.

'Hell! Look over there, Lyon. It's Indians,' shrieked Silverstone.

They jumped up, found their rifles and pulled back the hammer mechanism ready to fire. A hundred yards down the road, Little Bob turned to the sheriff.

'Well, they have seen us now and it don't look like they are going to vamoose.'

They were within twenty yards of the soldiers before Lyon recognized them and dropped the aim of his rifle.

'Sheriff, what are you doing dressed up in Indian clothes? You sure gave us a shock.'

As the troopers put down their rifles, Hickey enquired: 'So Langan's back in the ranch house, is he?'

'Yep, laid up in bed, but I heard from Maria that he's getting better. So that's good news. He's a real gentleman. Sends us out hot food every day,' replied Silverstone.

'Well, what do you think of that, Little Bob?' said Hickey. 'Ain't that the best news to hear he's getting right. Maybe we should just mosey up to the house and see him now that we are here.'

The sheriff's disingenuous comments

were in reality meant for the trooper's ears and they provoked the expected response from Lyon.

'I'm not sure we can allow you to do that, Sheriff. After all, it was you who shot him. For all we know you might be wanting to kill him.'

The sheriff laughed. 'I told Little Bob here that a fine pair of soldiers like yourselves would say that. He reckoned that I would have to kill you first.'

As soon as he finished speaking his hand dropped to his pistol. When they saw the grip, both soldiers dived to retrieve their rifles. But they never got anywhere near the guns. Hickey's pistol was released from its holster to discharge a bullet into the back of each of them.

Those shots alerted a number of people in different ways. Jack Langan was in his upstairs bedroom, being fed some soup by Rebecca. He immediately started to get up and only momentarily winced with pain. Next, Maria, who had been cleaning in the parlour, made for the front door to investigate the noise. When she opened it she blinked to check that her eyes were not deceiving her. But as she looked again she still saw the sheriff and his deputy riding down the drive at full gallop dressed up as Indians. She banged the door shut to lock and bolt it. When after a few moments she heard the sound of a heavy boot crashing against the wooden frame, she pulled over a large oak table and stacked that up against the door.

Then remembering the layout of the house, she ran down the hall to secure the back door. Just as she was about to reach it she saw the handle turning and the space between the door and its frame growing larger. In stepped Little Bob, grinning inanely at her. She let out a long high-pitched shout that was abruptly truncated when the deputy crashed the butt of his rifle against her jaw. As she slumped to the floor, Little Bob stepped over her and roughly pulled the keys out of her hand. He then locked the door, turning the key twice in the lock to ensure that that would not be used as an escape route and went to allow the waiting sheriff entrance at the front of the house.

As soon as he crossed the threshold, Hickey shouted up the staircase:

'We know that you are up there, Langan. You hear me. It's time to finish it all.'

No reply came and Hickey once more screamed at the top of his voice:

'OK. We'll play it your way.'

From the bundle that he was cradling in his arms, he handed a couple of torches to Little Bob. Rods with rags that had been soaked in the paraffin that they kept in the jailhouse for their lamps. The sheriff struck a match and lit them. At first just a smear of smoke arose but in only a few seconds, bright orange flames started to leap into the air. The lawmen split up and went into the various downstairs rooms to allow these flames to court and caress the thick curtains that hung around each window. Then the blazing torches encouraged the fire to consume the old wooden furniture that adorned the ranch house. Wherever the flames were teasingly stroked against a cabinet or a chair or a desk, they would start to turn it black and then with a crack it would be alight, signalling an all-consuming marriage between that piece of furniture and the raging inferno. Upstairs, behind the bedroom door, Jack and Rebecca heard the loud cracks made by the voracious flames and smelled the pungent odour of burning.

The last person to be alerted was Edmund. Jack Langan had insisted that after his ordeal he should stay around the ranch house instead of going off on roundups with the other cowboys. That morning he was in a clearing about a quarter of a mile behind the ranch house, cutting up firewood. Maisie had chosen to accompany him and was sitting on an old tree-trunk, humming to herself. When he heard the shots, he told his wife to wait, picked up his shotgun and sprinted for the house. He arrived at the back door and after a futile effort to open it, ran around the house. He was surprised to see the front door lying wide open but he felt the heat of the flames as soon as he approached. Without thinking, he dashed inside and tore through the thick black smoke to reach the kitchen where he came across Maria lying on the floor, still unconscious. He knew then that the fire was not the result of an accident nor the shots unrelated. He lowered his shotgun and closed his forefinger around both triggers.

He started back up the hallway, this time progressing much more slowly and cautiously. But Little Bob, moving from one room to another, saw him first. The smoke made identification difficult but when, through squinting eyes, he recognized Edmund, he dropped his torch in amazement.

'You're dead. You are a ghost,' he screamed in unison with the bang from the twin barrels of the shotgun being fired. The force lifted Little Bob right off his feet and slammed him against a wall before his body slumped lifeless to the floor.

'Ain't no phantom that can fire a blunderbuss like that,' said Edmund to himself. Smoke had started to lodge in the back of his throat, causing him to cough and splutter. In a frantic search for better air he dropped to the floor and started to crawl on his hands and knees towards the main staircase. Then he froze as he saw a pair of brown leather boots come out of the parlour. He looked up and against an illuminated backdrop, recognized the sheriff holding a handkerchief tightly over his mouth and nostrils. Edmund saw the gun in the other hand but realized that partly because of the smoke and partly because he was on the ground, the sheriff had failed to spot him.

He started to scurry back on hands and knees towards the kitchen, but Billy Bob heard the noise and fired. Then a familiar voice, weaker than he remembered it but still comforting, sounded through the air. It came from somewhere on the staircase.

'Hickey!'

The sheriff spun around and above him on the mezzanine, holding his weakened body steady by gripping one hand tightly against the banister, stood Langan, pistol already drawn in the other hand. Rebecca, who had helped him out of bed and supported him down the stairs against all of her instincts, had been pushed roughly aside when they saw the fire from the sheriff's gun rip through the darkness. She cowered against the wall and the cold sweat of fear contrasted with the heat from the flames that she could feel redden her cheeks. This time there was no doubt in Langan's mind about his intended action; there would be no compunction or self-recrimination over the result. Langan shot as soon as he had spoken and the bullet punched the sheriff in the side. Hickey fired off two shots in the general direction of his adversary. Both bullets ploughed into the finial on top of the post that held the staircase at the mezzanine and splinters of wood were sent flying into the air. The one shot that was returned out of the blackness confirmed he had not managed to kill his Nemesis yet.

Hickey was sweating profusely from the heat of the conflagration and the smoke was billowing in thicker and thicker clouds. He put his hand over his jacket and felt the warm blood ooze out of the hole that Langan's bullet had punctured. It was time to leave and let the fire do the job for which it had been raised.

From the shelter of the wall Hickey fired two shots in the general direction of the staircase. That would keep Langan doubting, he reckoned. Give him enough time to dash the few yards to the front door and outside he would find a cool comforting breeze. He took the key from the inside lock as he passed through the entrance, took a deep breath of fresh air and pulled the door tightly towards him. When he had turned the key in the lock, he stuffed it deep inside the pocket of his breeches. He watched the flames leap out of the roof. All of the trapped occupants would soon be charred in the conflagration. No way out, both doors locked and the keys removed. No escape. No evidence would be left. Even the evidence by association, Little Bob's body, would be totally cremated and unrecognizable. He failed, though, to see Hayin and four braves standing behind the barn as he rode off.

Inside the house Langan and Rebecca reached the bottom of the stairs and saw Edmund crawl around a pile of rubble. He got to the front door and pulled away the table before twisting the handle. 'No good this way,' he shouted back. 'It's locked and the key's gone. Back door too. Get on the floor, it's easier to breathe.'

In the kitchen they found Maria just regaining consciousness in time for her to realize the danger she was facing from the flames. Although her lungs were competing with the fire for oxygen she found sufficient air to let out a scream amplified by hysteria.

'It's alright, Maria. They've gone away and we'll get out of here, believe me,' assured Langan. But even as the words tripped out of his mouth, he was starting to doubt what he was saying.

'What about the windows?' he screamed at Edmund.

'No, no good. They set fire to the curtains to block off the windows. Fire's too fierce in any of the rooms down here. Only hope is getting back upstairs and out of one of the bedroom windows.'

Just as they reached the hall they saw the wooden staircase being completely engulfed in the fire and heard the crash as the steps at the top gave way. Langan put his arm over his face to protect himself from the flaming splinters of wood that were showering down on them and also to hide his crestfallen countenance from his companions as his heart sank. Then, they all heard a loud thud at the door, then another and a third even louder that shook the very walls of the house.

They could not have guessed that on the other side of that heavy portal, four Indians had found a long log and using it like a battering ram were banging it against the door. The raised porch meant that they had only two or three steps in their run-up, but they put every sinew of their bodies into that charge and on the fourth contact, the lock sprang open and the door fell back.

Flames rushed out, drawn by the draught of the air and the Indians felt the heat of the conflagration. But still they jumped over the oak barrier and guided the occupants to safety. Rebecca and Maria were unceremoniously thrown over a back and carried. Langan was supported under each shoulder by a brave and Edmund made his own way towards a place on the front yard where the burning heat no longer pained their flesh. His wife was standing there waiting for him, praying for another salvation.

In that wonderful daylight surrounded by air that would not claw at the back of his throat nor sting his eyes, Langan sat on the ground. He stopped coughing and spluttering long enough to confirm that they were all safe, then look up as Hayin approached.

'The horse soldiers will be here very soon,' the medicine man said. 'We must go before they arrive.'

'No, wait. Things are different from the last time I spoke to the major. We know for certain now that it was the sheriff who set fire to the ranch house.'

The Indian spoke again. 'They will see two of their own lying dead and grow angry. I am still not sure that their chief will want to believe you, so we shall go to the place where we first came across the Buffalo and wait to hear their word.'

As they rode away, Rebecca helped Langan to stand. They watched the fire bring the last structures of the ranch house tumbling to the ground. Both Rebecca and Langan understood that a chapter in their respective lives was coming swiftly to an end. Another one was about to begin.

20

Kaisen had ensured that he had the fastest mount available and so the rest of the troop were having some difficulty keeping up with his pace as he led them towards the smoke. They were approaching the bridge when he saw on the other side of the water, a single Indian slumped over his horse and proceeding at a slow deliberate trot. They would have converged just at the river had the solitary rider not looked up and seen the cavalry. He immediately changed direction, cutting off at a right angle and heading up the steep incline. Kaisen watched him as he waited for Nichol to catch up.

'Lieutenant,' he said, 'you and a few of the men come with me and we'll catch that varmint. Find out what he's running away from in such a hurry. The rest of the troop carry on down to the ranch house and find the other ones. Tell them not to be shy about shooting them if they don't surrender.'

The major did not delay after he had barked his order but galloped on at full speed. The hoofs of his horse were clattering against the wooden slats of the bridge by the time that Nichol had disengaged two soldiers and relayed the remainder of Kaisen's instructions.

The lone horseman appeared to be going slower and slower as the steepness of the hill increased and Kaisen was catching up with him. The major pulled out his pistol and fired twice in rapid succession. In spite of army regulations, he favoured a Smith & Wesson Schofield because the break-open design made it easier to reload on horseback. The second shot hit the pursued horse in the rump and it reared up, its hoofs clawing at empty air. This unexpected jolt forced Hickey to release his already weak grip and he found himself slowly but surely sliding off the animal's backside.

As soon as he stopped rolling on the ground his sense of self-preservation charged to the fore. More adrenaline than he had ever experienced before pumped through his veins and he no longer felt the heat of Langan's bullet. Kaisen had just about reached him and was preparing to shot again when he recognized Hickey's contorted face looking up at him. He pulled on the reins with all of his might and as the horse's legs reacted to the force on the bridle, the question of why Hickey was wearing buckskins pushed the intention to shoot from the forefront of his conscious thought. His mouth opened.

'Hickey, what the devil . . . ' he started to shout.

But the sheriff's shot prevented the full expression of the major's confusion. The bullet could not have been better placed, straight between the eyes. Kaisen's body was hurled out of the saddle and with a dust-spreading bang it landed motionless on the ground. Hickey had no time to admire his accuracy. He could hear the hoofs of his second pursuer pounding up the hill towards him. He turned and pulled the hammer back on his revolver.

Nichol had already calculated that the speed of the gallop and the uneven ground would not guarantee an accurate shot. Instead he had unsheathed his sword. As he rode at full speed past Hickey the heavy-bladed sabre in the cavalryman's hand was swung down and cut into the sheriff's chest with consummate ease. When it hit the breastbone, the force sent a shiver up through the steel and Nichol felt a strange tingling in his fingers. He opened his palm and rode on empty handed until he could slow his horse sufficiently to allow him to jump off. The sheriff was still standing and his gun continued to point towards Nichol. He fired but the bullet went harmlessly skywards before the sheriff pirouetted and collapsed in a ghoulish ballet. His body now flat against the ground still held the sword, like a plinth proudly displaying a trophy. As the lieutenant ran back the other two soldiers had reached the bodies.

'Major Kaisen's dead, sir,' shouted the first soldier.

Nichol nodded as the second soldier stood up.

'Lieutenant, this here ain't no Indian,' the man exclaimed. 'It's that sheriff down in Franklin.'

'That doesn't completely surprise me, trooper.' Then he said in a more authoritative voice: 'Come on, let's get mounted up again. There isn't anything more that we can do here. We'll come back for the bodies once we find out what's happening.'

The rest of the troop had reached the ranch and found the bodies of Lyon and Silverstone. In spite of the raging fire just ahead of them, the soldiers dismounted and proceeded on foot up the drive. They found only five dishevelled figures, all but one with soot-blackened faces and hands, standing together and smiling broadly. The men in the blue serge uniforms were confounded by this group appearing to be so happy in such circumstances.

'Are you folks OK? How long ago did the Indians leave?' shouted Sergeant Murphy.

Langan stared for a moment at the soldiers now rushing around, gathering up buckets of water and shovels of dirt that they could use to quell the inferno. He let his eyes rest on the three golden stripes still shining out against the blue of the uniform as the sergeant trembled.

'Hell. We sure didn't expect them redskin varmints to be attacking ranches like this.'

Langan shook his head and with a voice hoarse from inhaling smoke, said:

'They didn't attack us, Sergeant. They saved us. If it wasn't for your so called redskin varmints we would all be going up in smoke just like that house.'

'So where are they now and who set fire to the place?'

Langan was wondering which question he should answer first when he saw three horsemen gallop into the yard. He recognized Lieutenant Nichol and cast a warm smile over to him as he dismounted.

'Thing's under control, Sergeant?' enquired the officer as he moved to join the conversation.

'Yes sir,' snapped Murphy. 'Ain't no other buildings close enough, so the fire should burn itself out given time and we'll help it along a bit with water and dirt.'

Murphy was looking over Nichol's shoulder as he spoke, then his curiosity found voice.

'Major Kaisen, sir? He isn't with you. Something up?'

'The major's dead, I'm afraid, Sergeant. I'm the next senior officer, so I'll be taking over again.'

Langan strained to hear the conversation as Murphy asked: 'Dead, sir. What happened?'

'We'll go into the details later. For

now though you just need to know that it wasn't an Indian who killed him. So after we put the fire out, we are going to stand down. No more chasing them around the country. We'll go back to camp and await further orders.'

As Murphy saluted and went off to convey the information to his men, Nichol took Langan by the hand and shook it.

'Hickey's dead as well. We killed him trying to escape from here. Still wearing Indian clothes. Well done, Mr Langan. You finally did it. You proved that it wasn't the Indians that killed your father.'

The following day at dawn, Nichol set out from camp with only a handful of men to accompany him. When he reached the mouth of the canyon, he told the soldiers to make camp and wait for him. And then, holding a standard aloft with a white handkerchief fluttering in the slight breeze, he slowly trotted into the cavernous gap. He had followed the rough track on the floor of the canyon for about a mile when he heard the incongruous call of an owl. He knew instinctively that it had not been made by any nocturnal bird but he could see nothing when he looked behind him. He turned around again to resume his progress and was startled to see only a few feet in front of his horse's nose an Indian standing legs astride and arms folded. He looked at the ostentatious headdress of eagle feathers and the colourful paint on his face.

'Hayin?' he enquired.

'That is what I call myself in the presence of white men. You are Lieutenant Nichol. I have heard that you are a fair man.'

The lieutenant dismounted and when the Indian sat cross-legged on the ground, he did likewise. The soldier looked deep into the Indian's face but did not see trust.

'Your braves are around here some-where?' he asked.

Hayin waved his hands at the sun-bleached walls of rock.

'They wait in the stone. They are there to see that no other soldiers come.'

'OK, I guess that you don't have a lot of reason to trust us. But I have to tell you that you have broken the treaty between my government and the Shoshone people by leaving the reservation.'

'The braves who wait in the rocks are young men with adventure in their hearts and ideas in their heads. They belong to a people that has for centuries wandered these plains following the buffalo and the deer. My people know that they have broken the covenant. That's why I was sent to find them and bring them back. They will not go unpunished but they will be dealt with by a council of Shoshone elders. They have interfered in the world of the white man only once and that was to save the life of a good man.'

'You have already proved that you are a man of your word. If you let me lead the braves back to their village then I promise you that I shall ask the government to take no other action.'

Two days later the party had reached the forest that marked the start of the reservation. From their high vantage point they could see over the treetops to the point where the plain started again and saw in the distance smoke rising out of the roofs of a clutch of tepees. They stopped and Hayin motioned to Nichol to come closer.

'Look, down below. That is the village from where these braves came. Their women will be waiting for them.'

Nichol held out his open palm and the Indian looked at it. Tentatively he reached across and placed his own hand in it. The two men tightened their grip and saw in each other a shared desire to live in peace. Then the Indians began the descent down the hillside, by themselves. Nichol turned the soldiers around and headed back. As they crossed the hill road that overlooked Far Fields, the lieutenant pulled his horse to a halt and surveyed the scene below him. Two dozen men were hard at work. They had already cleared the ashes of the old house and were in the process of digging in new foundations. The air resonated with a cacophony of nails being hammered into wood and timber being sawed into planks.

In the midst of all this activity, Rebecca was shouting directions. Then she caught sight of Langan trying to coax a team of two horses to pull a large uprooted tree. He was having limited success, however, and she laughed out loud at the lack of equine co-operation he was achieving. Edmund, shaking his head, came across to take the bridle from Langan's hand and simultaneously slap the lead horse on the rump. As the team moved off dragging the wood behind it, Langan approached Rebecca.

'See, I told you I wasn't cut out to be a rancher,' he said. 'Maybe it's time I thought about going back East and doing something that I'm good at.'

Immediately, she looked crestfallen.

'Going back? I was kind of hoping that you had abandoned the idea of going back. You are exactly the sort of man that we need in Idaho. Good and brave. You don't need to rope steers or build houses, we need good lawyers too. Folk who can drive this Territory into a State, a place that we can all be proud of.'

'To be honest,' he replied, 'I've realized lately that even though I get on that train I will never really be able to leave this place. Too many things have happened to me here.' He looked at her, wondering whether she would be able to realize her part in the changes that he had experienced.

'Don't get the train then. Stay here with me. This new house can be for the both of us. You must realize that I've fallen in love with you?'

Langan grabbed her hand and repeated with astonishment:

'Fallen in love with me?'

'Yes,' she confirmed. 'When you were lying on the ground with Hickey's bullets in you I realized that even if Pat as a young man had been there, it would have been you that I would have come to. Do you love me?'

'Rebecca, I started to fall in love with you the day that I met you, but when you placed yourself between me and Hickey's gun, I also knew that I wanted to spend the rest of my life with you. I will stay here, but on one condition.'

'What's that?' she asked through a seductive smile.

'Marry me.'

The wedding was held in the new house and it was the first time in his life that Edmund had been a best man.

THE END

We do hope that you have enjoyed reading this large print book.

Did you know that all of our titles are available for purchase?

We publish a wide range of high quality large print books including:
Romances, Mysteries, Classics
General Fiction
Non Fiction and Westerns

Special interest titles available in large print are:
The Little Oxford Dictionary
Music Book, Song Book
Hymn Book, Service Book

Also available from us courtesy of Oxford University Press:
Young Readers' Dictionary
(large print edition)
Young Readers' Thesaurus
(large print edition)

For further information or a free brochure, please contact us at:
Ulverscroft Large Print Books Ltd.,
The Green, Bradgate Road, Anstey,
Leicester, LE7 7FU, England.
Tel: (00 44) **0116 236 4325**
Fax: (00 44) **0116 234 0205**

Other titles in the
Linford Western Library:

THE HIGH COUNTRY YANKEE

Elliot Conway

Joel Garretson quit his job as Chief of Scouts to travel to Texas and claim his piece of land. He needed to forget the killings he had seen — and done — fighting the Sioux and the Crow in Montana . . . But he soon has to confront Texas *pistoleros* and then, aided by a bunch of ex-Missouri brush boys, he faces the task of rescuing two women held by *comancheros* in their stronghold . . . In the territory of the Llana Estacado, New Mexico, the violent blood-letting will commence . . .